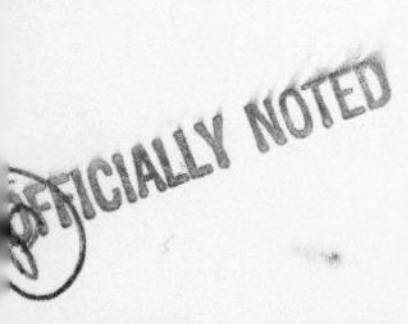
OFFICIALLY NOTED

INSPECTOR WEST AT HOME

INSPECTOR WEST AT HOME

JOHN CREASEY

Charles Scribner's Sons / New York

First American Edition, 1973

1 3 5 7 9 11 13 15 17 19 C/C 20 18 16 14 12 10 8 6 4 2

Printed in the United States of America
Library of Congress Catalog Card Number 73–1114
SBN 684–13396–2 (cloth)

Contents

1

Roger West Has a Day Off

Superintendent Abbott inserted his tall figure and expressionless face into the narrow opening of the door of the Chief Inspector's office on B Floor at New Scotland Yard. Abbott seemed never to enter a door in natural fashion, but to slide in as if he were anxious to be unobserved.

When Roger West, who was in the office with Chief Inspector Eddie Day, looked up and saw the vacant face of the Superintendent, his heart dropped. He had schemed to take this particular day off, because it was his wife's birthday, but he had been pessimistic until, when he had arrived an hour before, he had found a note from Abbott telling him to give details of one or two reports and go off. It was a dull, grey day, with early April making a passable imitation of late November; lights were burning over the desks furthest from the windows.

At the Yard, they called Abbott the Apostle of Gloom, for he was invariably the bearer of evil tidings, which perhaps accounted for his cold, vacuous expression.

Eddie Day looked up, pushed his chair back, and grinned. Eddie was not handsome, and when he grinned he showed most of his prominent front teeth.

"Oh, West," said Abbott. "Will you be at home this afternoon?"

Roger looked puzzled. "I expect so, yes."

"Can you make sure that you will be in?"

“I had thought of doing a show with my wife, but that wouldn’t be until this evening.” Abbott was not a man with whom it was wise to take liberties. “You’re not going to bring me back, are you?”

“I just wanted to be sure where I could find you,” Abbott promptly effaced himself, closing the door without a sound.

“What a ruddy nerve!” Eddie declared. “Trying to put you in a fix so’s you don’t know what to do. I’ll tell you what, Handsome, take Janet out and let Abbott get someone else to chase round after him.” Eddie, who was a shrewd officer and at his particular job—the detection of forgery—head and shoulders above anyone else at the Yard, still looked and talked like a detective-sergeant newly promoted from a beat. “Cold as a fish, that’s what I always think the Apostle is.” Then he frowned at Roger’s expression. “Say, what’s biting you, Handsome? You look as if you’ve eaten something that don’t agree with you.”

“It’s nothing,” said Roger. “He might have given me one day without wanting me on tap.” He locked his desk and took his hat and mackintosh from a hat-stand. “Head him off for me if you can, Eddie.”

“Trust me,” said Eddie. “I won’t let you down. Give my love to Janet!”

His laughter echoed in Roger’s ears as he went out, and walked thoughtfully along the passage.

A soft drizzle of rain, a mist which threatened to become fog and a sky of a uniform dull grey did not depress him. He slipped into a shop, for Janet, and contemplated an afternoon in front of a log fire after a good lunch at a favorite Chelsea restaurant.

When he reached his small detached house in Bell Street, Chelsea, she was waiting in the lounge in a gaily-coloured mackintosh. She was tucking in a few stray curls of her dark hair beneath a wide-brimmed felt hat.

“Will I do, darling?”

Slowly, Roger West looked her up and down. As slowly, he began to smile. The wicked gleam in his eyes brought a flush to Janet’s cheeks.

"You ass!" she exclaimed.

"Yes, you'll do," declared Roger. "Although why we want to go out I don't know. I'd much rather stay in. Catch!" He tossed the package to her.

She caught the package, moved to him and kissed him. "I thought we said 'no presents, only a day out,' " she said. "Roger, you haven't got to go back?"

He laughed at her sudden alarm. "Not as far as I know. That's not a peace-offering!"

Yet as she opened the present he wished that she had not reminded him of the Yard.

Janet enthused over a locknit twin set, then suddenly dropped the set on a table. A few minutes later, with her hair slightly rumpled and faint smears of lipstick on his lips and cheeks, Roger had completely forgotten Abbott.

Throughout the meal, at the French restaurant ten minutes walk from the house, they talked of trifles. Only when they were in the lounge drinking coffee, and Roger could see into the street, did a frown darken his face.

"What's the matter?" asked Janet.

"Nothing," said Roger.

"Darling," said Janet, "you can probably deceive all the criminals in the world but it's no use lying to me. What did you see?"

"Now would I lie to you?" asked Roger. "I caught a glimpse of Tiny Martin outside and wondered why he's here. He's been on a job at Bethnal Green."

"Who's Tiny Martin?"

"A sergeant who does Abbott's leg work," said Roger. "Let's forget him."

But Martin was not so easily forgotten. He was a tall, thin, cadaverous-looking man who always worked with Abbott and had something of the Superintendent's strange coldness.

In spite of the drizzle, Roger and Janet sauntered along the Chelsea Embankment before returning to Bell Street. Twice Roger caught a glimpse of Martin, although Janet had completely forgotten the man and was busy speculating on Roger's chances of a month's holiday so that they could go abroad. They were still discussing it when they reached the house. He thought that he caught a glimpse of Martin at the end of the road, but dismissed the idea and went indoors. He sat back in an easy chair and told himself that he was both a happy man and a lucky one. He looked a little drawn—Janet knew that overwork explained it, but although there was a tinge of grey at his temples he looked absurdly young to be a Chief Inspector at the Yard. Their closest friend, Mark Lessing, frequently declared that Roger amazed him, so rarely did good looks and a keen mind go together.

"What time must we leave?" Janet asked.

"We shouldn't start later than six," said Roger, "the curtain rises at a quarter past seven and I don't suppose we'll be able to get a cab." He reached out for his cup and then sat upright, hearing footsteps on the front path. The lounge was at the front of the house.

The footsteps were heavy and deliberate.

"Darling, why are you on edge so?" demanded Janet. "It's probably the laundryman." She put the lid over a dish of toasted crumpets and hurried to the front door. Roger glanced towards the hall, not knowing himself why he felt so worked up, until he heard Abbott's familiar voice.

"Good afternoon," said the Superintendent, "is Inspector West in, please?"

"Yes, he's at home," said Janet, her tone reflecting the keenness of her disappointment.

"Ask him to be good enough to spare me a few minutes, will you? I am Superintendent Abbott of New Scotland Yard."

"Yes, I know," said Janet. She asked Abbott into the hall, then came to tell Roger, who was standing up and sipping his tea.

"Shall I ask him in here?"

"Yes, you'd better," said Roger, reluctantly.

"I suppose I'll have to offer him some tea," said Janet. She made a moué and went out into the hall again, but she sounded brighter as she invited Abbott to come into the lounge.

"It is a private matter, Mrs. West. I would rather see him alone," Abbott said.

Roger went into the hall with a manner which could hardly be called inviting.

"Wouldn't a phone call have done as well?" He was on surer ground in his home than at the Yard. He saw Detective Sergeant Martin standing by the gate, looking gloomier because it was raining harder. Drops fell from the turned-down brim of his trilby. Roger frowned and added more sharply: "What is it?"

Deliberately, Abbott wiped his feet on the door-mat and shook the rain from his hat into the porch before placing it on the hall-stand. Janet closed the door. Abbott did not take off his mackintosh as he said:

"I'd like a word with you, West, alone."

Tight-lipped, Roger led the way to the dining-room. He stood aside for Abbott to pass and the Superintendent sidled in.

Roger waited as Abbott regarded him with narrowed eyes; he was a spare man with a curiously fleshless face and lips which were almost colorless.

"Well, what is it?" Roger's exasperation got the better of his discretion.

"I think you know why I've called," said Abbott.

"I certainly don't," Roger said. "And I hope it won't take long. Is it the Micklejohn case?"

"It is not," Abbott said. "West, I don't wish to make this more unpleasant than I have to. You know why I've come and your aggressive attitude won't help you."

Roger stared. "Aggressive attitude?" he echoed. "If you mean a reasonable annoyance at being visited at home when I'm off duty—"

"I mean nothing of the kind," said Abbott, and sighed, as if what he had to say was extremely distasteful. "I've come, of course, to search your house."

Roger looked at him stupidly. "You've come to—" he began,

then stopped abruptly. He was no longer angry, but was utterly puzzled. "I wish you'd tell me what all this is about. It's got past the joking stage."

Abbott pushed his hand into his coat and drew out a folded slip of paper. There was something uncomfortably familiar about it—an official search warrant. Even when it was upside down he recognized the flourishes of the signature of Sir Guy Chatworth, the then Assistant Commissioner at the Yard, but until he had read it he did not really believe that it authorized Abbott to search *his* house. He drew in a deep breath, dropped the warrant on the dining-table and said:

"I think you owe me an explanation. I have no idea what this is all about."

Abbott did not immediately answer and before Roger could speak again, still shocked by Abbott's announcement, a second knock came at the front door and Janet's footsteps followed. He paid little attention to what was happening outside, but looked into Abbott's narrowed eyes and tried to quieten the heavy thumping of his heart.

2

A Policeman Under a Shadow

"It is not a pleasant task for me to present this warrant and I think you should stop pretending that you know nothing about it," said Abbott.

"I tell you I haven't the faintest idea," insisted Roger.

"Hallo, Jan!" cried a man from the hall. Roger recognized the voice of a close friend, Mark Lessing. Abbott was so surprised that he looked towards the door and Mark continued: "How's the birthday party going?" There was a smacking sound and then, in a gasping voice, Janet said:

"Mark, you ass!"

"Now what is a kiss between friends on a birthday?" demanded Lessing. "Especially on the twenty-first—it *is* your twenty-first, isn't it?"

Abbott pinched his nostrils. "Well, West?" he said.

Roger was thanking the fates for sending Mark Lessing just then. Mark had given him time to realize that he would be wise to adopt a less hostile attitude. There was some absurd mistake, but it could be rectified.

So he forced a smile.

"I haven't anything to say about it, Superintendent, except that I'm completely at a loss." His attempt to be affable faded out in the face of Abbott's cold stare. "Obviously you must have some reason for getting a warrant sworn for me."

"You *must* know the reason," insisted Abbott.

Roger fancied that the faint emphasis on the "must" implied a query. Before he could speak again, however, there came from the lounge an astonishing sound—astonishing because of the previous quiet. It was the deep, throbbing bass notes of the piano. Almost at once Mark began to sing, more loudly than harmoniously. A suspicion entered Roger's mind: that Mark was drunk.

"Is that din necessary?" Abbott demanded irritably.

"Is any of this necessary?" asked Roger, tartly. "I thought I was going to have a day off. I'm taking my wife to a show as I told you. Are you serious about executing this warrant?"

"Of course I'm serious."

"Why did you get it?" demanded Roger.

He had to raise his voice to make himself heard for Mark was going wild. He crashed wrong note after wrong note and he was thumping so heavily that the piano frame was quivering and groaning.

"If you will stop that noise I will tell you," said Abbott. He stepped to the door. Roger had to go with him. When it was open, the whole house seemed to be in uproar, and he heard a bump upstairs.

Then he pushed open the lounge door.

Janet was by the mantelpiece, doubled up with laughter, for Mark was playing with idiotic abandon. As he crashed his hands on the keys he bobbed his head and his dark hair fell over his forehead; after each note he raised his hand high into the air, flexing his wrist. His pale face was flushed and his eyes were glistening.

"What the devil do you think you're doing?" Roger demanded, striding across the room and grabbing Mark's shoulder. "Stop it, you fool!" Mark continued, bobbing his head up and down vigorously. *Boom!* went the C sharp and then Mark played a run superbly. *Boom!* went the A, then G sharp, then C again.

"West, I insist that you stop this nonsense!" called Abbott.

Boom! went Mark. Then he took his hands from the keys and swung round on the piano stool, pushed his hair out of his eyes and glared at Abbott. Roger had never seen him look so furious.

"Nonsense?" he roared at Abbott. "Who the hell are you, sir? What do you mean by calling my playing *nonsense?* If you have no appreciation of good music, if your ignorance is so abysmal, I advise you *not* to declare it to the world. Is *this* what you would call nonsense?" He swung round to the piano, raised his hands and began to crash out Liszt's *Liebesträume*.

Abbott stared, tight-lipped. Roger, at first irritated by Janet's laughter, saw an expression in her eyes which gave him his first inkling that she knew why Mark was playing the fool. She began to laugh again as if she couldn't stop, and Abbott looked about desperately; Roger thought he bellowed "madhouse." He did shout loudly enough to be heard above the playing: "Stop him, West!"

Roger tried, half-heartedly, beginning to wonder whether Mark could possibly be making this din deliberately, as a distraction. Roger remembered the bump upstairs. His confusion grew worse but he made a good show of losing his temper. Mark stopped at last and rose disdainfully from the piano. He brushed his hair back from his forehead and straightened his tie—and then he jumped, as if horrified.

At no time handsome, he was a distinguished-looking man with a high forehead, a Roman nose and a pointed chin; his lips were shapely and his complexion so good that it was almost feminine. About him there was an air, normally, of arrogance. Just then his whole expression was of horror.

"My sainted Cousin Lot!" he exclaimed. "Superintendent Abbott! Why didn't someone tell me? I *am* sorry. I'd no idea it was you." He continued to stare into the Superintendent's eyes while uttering abject apologies. Since he was not a policeman they were excessive, but he was known at the Yard as a friend of "Handsome" West's who dabbled in crime. "You know, Superintendent," he went on in the same shocked tones, "I was absolutely carried away. I've been working hard and just felt like letting my hair down. Something powerful in the way of urges. And it's Janet's birthday. I remembered that this afternoon and rushed over to apologize for not having wished her many happy returns. I say, Jan, could you rustle up a cup of tea and a biscuit?"

"Of course," said Janet. "Will you stay to tea, Superintendent?"

Abbott had listened to Mark's protestations, his face gradually resuming a stony aspect. He turned to Janet, obviously ill-at-ease. Roger offered him a cigarette.

"Don't get worried, sir," he said. "All this will work itself out. Why don't you have a cup of tea and talk about it?"

"What's this?" demanded Mark. "Sticky business on the criminal stakes? Famous member of the Big Five flummoxed, Handsome West called in to get his nose on the trail?"

"You're not going to take Roger away!" Janet protested. Abbott had the grace to cough in confusion.

Roger put him out of his misery.

"Not in the usual way, Jan, anyhow. I don't know what's gone wrong, but he's turned up with a search-warrant. I must be credited with having broken open a till."

"A search-warrant?" gasped Mark.

"What?" cried Janet.

Roger thought that they put a shade more emphasis than was needed. Abbott appeared to think their amazement understandable and sincere; he coughed again.

"You can't be serious!" exclaimed Janet.

"I am afraid I am, Mrs. West," said Abbott. "I really must not waste any more time." He shot a quick, almost furtive glance at Roger. "Information has been lodged to the effect that you received, today, a sum of money intended as a bribe in consideration of withholding action against a criminal when you knew that action was required."

Roger stared, blankly.

"Let's be serious," said Mark. "A joke is a joke and I like one with any man, but this—"

"It is no joking matter," Abbott assured him. "But for the peculiar circumstances, I would not have made the statement in this room. However, you appear to wish your wife to know. That is your responsibility."

Janet stepped to Roger's side.

"*Is* he serious, Roger?"

Roger forced a smile. "Yes, he has a warrant, but it's coming to something when he adopts this method instead of a straightforward approach. I suppose he could have come while I was out instead of while I'm here, but apparently that's the extent of the consideration I can expect." He seemed almost amused. "It's all quite fantastic. It explains why Martin was dogging me, anyhow. He's probably been making sure I didn't pass the bribe on to anyone else!"

Abbott regarded him coldly.

"I can see nothing amusing in the situation, West."

"I suppose not," said Roger, dryly. "Hadn't you better start searching? You'll want to begin on us, but that doesn't include my wife."

"If it is necessary to search Mrs. West—and I hope it will not be—I hardly need tell you the proper measures will be taken. Will you be good enough to call in Martin and the others?"

"Others?"

"There are two detective-officers with him."

Roger nodded curtly, went to the front door and called the sergeant and his men. One of the plainclothes men was obviously embarrassed, but that didn't stop him from doing his job properly.

The police finished downstairs and went up. Roger heard the heavy movements of the men upstairs and thought how often he had been on exactly the same quest.

He had searched with a thoroughness which had brought the tension of the people waiting in another part of the house to breaking point. He had worked with a grim determination to find some evidence of complicity in crime and to break his victim's resistance. After the search, if it proved successful, came the arrest, the charge, the magistrate's court, the gradual collection and piecing together of evidence, the final day of the assize trial. That last stage was often absurdly short in view of the weary weeks of preparations which had preceded it. Jury, judge, sentence—and prison.

He could not really grasp that this was happening to him. Instead of being the Apostle of Gloom, Abbott became the Apostle of Doom. For with every minute which passed one thing became more obvious. The Superintendent would not have come here, and Chatworth would not have signed the warrant, unless they felt convinced that they would find evidence that he had accepted bribes.

He lit a cigarette and stared at Janet helplessly. Her lips curved in an encouraging smile.

The men were still moving about upstairs and time was flying; it was a quarter past five. Every minute worsened the suspense.

Janet turned restlessly towards the window.

"How much longer will they be?"

"Not long," Roger said.

Mark broke in, reassuringly.

"After all, no news is good news. If they'd found the alleged evidence they would have come down by now."

Almost as he spoke, footsteps sounded on the stairs.

The three turned towards the door, and only the plainclothes man seemed indifferent. All of the search party appeared to be coming and Roger, feeling a curious mixture of relief and tension, stared at the door handle. Someone spoke in a low-pitched voice but the handle did not turn. The front door opened and footsteps scraped on the narrow gravel path.

Roger muttered a sharp imprecation, stepped towards the door and opened it. Abbott was standing at the foot of the stairs.

"Well?" The word almost choked Roger.

"I want you to believe that I'm really sorry about this," Abbott said. His lips moved so little that he looked incapable of feeling. He glanced towards the open door, and Roger, following his gaze, saw a woman approaching with Sergeant Martin. He recognized the newcomer as a tall, round-faced, jovial policewoman, one of the few female detectives at the Yard. Her purpose was only too apparent. He turned back to Abbott and spoke in a low-pitched, angry voice.

"I won't forget this afternoon's work, Mr. Abbott."

"I am sorry," Abbott repeated, expressionlessly. "Will you explain to your wife?"

Roger turned on his heel. He caught Janet's eye as he returned to the room. She gave him the impression that she had heard Abbott and was half-prepared for what was coming.

"They want to search you," Roger said. "They've a woman officer outside, so they're not breaking any regulations."

The woman officer stood on the threshold, smiling as if it were the best joke in the world. She was the only one of the police who seemed untroubled by the situation. Roger was startled when she winked at him before going upstairs with Janet to the main bedroom. Abbott entered the lounge and stared at Roger.

"All right," Roger said. "Get on with it," and allowed himself to be searched, standing rigid, neither helping nor impeding Tiny Martin, whose every movement seemed to be reluctant. The contents of his pockets were set out in neat array on a corner of the tea-table, next to the muffins which were now cold and unappetizing, with congealed butter smeared on them. The fire had nearly gone out. Mark, suddenly waking out of a reverie, began to stoke it, putting on a few knobs of coal and two logs and using a small pair of bellows.

Tiny Martin finished and Roger looked at Abbott.

"Well, are you satisfied?" He could have crashed his fist into Abbott's face.

"There is nothing here," Abbott admitted. He took some brown paper and oddments of string from his pocket. "What was in this?"

Roger stared. "I don't know."

"It is addressed to you and it's registered," Abbott said. "What was in it?"

Roger stretched out a hand and took the paper. It was

familiar but nothing clicked in his mind at first. It was of good quality, with a typewritten address on a plain label. The postmark was blurred but, after some seconds of close scrutiny, he saw that it was franked December, although he could not distinguish the date. His face cleared and he handed it back, knowing both what had been in it when it had reached him and why Abbott had found it upstairs.

"It contained a Christmas present from my father," he said. "Two first editions of Scott."

"*Christmas!*" Abbott was stung to the ejaculation.

"It was tucked away in my drawer for some months," continued Roger, icily. "I took it out today and wrapped a birthday present for my wife in it. So it has quite pleasant associations. I carried it all the way from here to the Yard. It was folded up in my raincoat pocket when you saw me this morning. I went to *Estelle's* in Oxford Street and bought a twin set. For my wife," he added with a savage note in his voice. "Are there any more intimate details you want to know?"

"Now, West—" began Abbott.

"'Now West' be damned!" growled Roger. "This is an outrageous visit. I may be a policeman, but I have some rights in law."

Mark began to whistle a dirge. Roger swung round on him. "Is that necessary? The piano's still there."

"I was only trying to while away the time. Ah! Sounds of progress." Footsteps, this time of the women, sounded on the stairs. Janet was first and she hurried in.

"Nothing at all on my person!" she declared. "I must say the officer made a job of it. Mr. Abbott, perhaps you are satisfied now that my husband is not a renegade policeman?" She stared at the paper and snapped: "What are you doing with that?"

"He thinks the filthy lucre was wrapped up in it," said Roger. "I've been giving him the history of it. Next time I bring you a present I ought to wrap it in newspaper or it will be used as evidence against me." He thrust his hands in his pockets. Now that the search was over, except for this room, he felt much better. He insisted on staying while the room was searched methodically. Nothing was left out of place, perhaps because the work was done under Abbott's cold eyes. When the man had finished, Roger eyed Abbott steadily and, after a prolonged silence, asked:

"Well, what's the next shot in your locker?"

For the first time he wondered whether they would take him away.

3

The Remarkable Story of Pep Morgan

Had the police made any discovery there would have been a formal charge; although they had not, they could still ask him to go with them for questioning. Abbott seemed not to hear Roger's question but turned and motioned to Tiny Martin and the policeman; the woman detective had already gone. The lesser policemen went out and Martin closed the door.

Abbott looked even more discomfited.

"I don't propose to do anything else now, West, but—"

"Now wait a minute," protested Roger. "Either you give me a clear bill or I call for legal aid. I hope you realize that I can create the mother and father of a row."

"You would be ill-advised—" Abbott began.

"What you seem to have forgotten is that I'm a policeman too," interrupted Roger. "If there were any suspicions of a man at the Yard and I had charge of the case, I'd have the ordinary decency to tell him what allegations had been made, and ask him for an explanation. I would not burst into his house, risk upsetting his wife, accuse him—"

"I accused you of nothing."

"You charged me with nothing but you've accused me of a damned sight too much. I want a full explanation and an apology."

Abbott rubbed his chin, slowly.

"I think you had better come with me," he said.

"If you want me, get a warrant."

"Do I understand that you refuse to come with me?" Abbott demanded.

"You understand that I refuse to come to the Yard for questioning until I have had a more formal explanation of the reason for all this, and I've had a chance to get legal aid. That's the least you would do if I were an ordinary civilian."

Abbott's mouth closed like a trap.

He turned and, without nodding to Janet or Mark, sidled through the partly open door and then closed it. There were muffled footsteps in the hall before the front door also closed. Footsteps followed on the gravel path. Roger stepped to the window and saw the party disappearing towards King's Road.

Roger turned to face the room, his lips curved in a smile which held no amusement.

"Sweet, I'm terribly sorry," he said.

"Don't be an ass, *you* couldn't help it," said Janet. "If it had to happen I'm glad it was here."

"I'm not and before I'm through I'll let Chatworth know what I think. I might have expected it of Abbott, but not of Chatworth." He lit a cigarette and stared at the teapot.

"I'll make some tea," Mark volunteered, now very subdued.

He took up the teatray and went out. He had once lived at the Bell Street house for some months and was familiar with every room and, as he often said, he liked to amuse himself in the kitchen.

Janet came over and sat on the arm of Roger's chair.

"Feeling pretty grim?"

Roger said: "Damnable! I—but Jan, what's Mark been up to?" He gripped Janet's arm. "I'm so woolly-headed I forgot all about that rumpus. He sent you a tea set as a present, didn't he? I'm not dreaming, you did have the parcel this morning?"

"Yes," admitted Janet. "I was afraid you were going to say something about that before." She stood up, stepped to the mantelpiece and took down a small cup and saucer, a fragile, beautiful thing. Idly, she flicked it with her finger; the china rang sweet and clear. "This was just to hoodwink Abbott."

Roger said: "Did he know that Abbott would be here?"

"Yes."

"And that din—" Roger jumped to his feet and stared at her, his eyes blazing. "There *was* someone upstairs. I thought I heard a bump when he was playing the fool on the piano. Jan, what has Mark been up to?"

"I only know that he told me he was going to make the devil of a row and the more noise I made the better it would be. Abbott did scare me and except for Mark the only light relief was when that woman took me upstairs," Janet said. "She was a pet! She told me that she didn't know what Abbott was up to and if he thought you were involved in shady work he must be off his head. You know her, of course?"

Roger nodded. "She's Winnie Marchant." The loyalty of the policewoman cheered him up. "Come on," he said, "I'm going to wring the truth out of Mark."

Mark was leaning against the gas-stove, whistling gently, imitating the noise of the kettle, which was singing.

"Here it comes!" he said.

"Never mind making tea," Roger said. "Janet will do that. What brought you here?"

"Oh, my natural prescience," said Mark, airily. "I heard a little bird tell a story about Abbott and Tiny Martin being on Handsome's heels and I thought I would come and introduce a little light relief. Was I good?" He seemed hopeful. "If there's any damage to that A string, I'll have it put right at my expense."

Janet took the teapot from him.

"Talk, Mark," Roger ordered.

"I can't tell you any more, except that the little bird was Pep Morgan."

"Pep!" exclaimed Janet, swinging on her heels.

“Morgan?” echoed Roger. “Where does he come in?”

“The senior partner of Morgan and Morgan, Private Inquiry Agents telephoned me about half an hour before I arrived and told me to hurry over here,” Mark said. “He added I was to kick up the dickens of a shindy if I found Abbott on the premises. Had it been anyone else but Pep I would have told him to take his practical jokes elsewhere, but Pep wouldn't play the fool. When I asked him why he told me to listen carefully if I wanted to save Handsome from Dartmoor. What else could I do but obey?”

Roger said slowly: “He must have had an idea of what Abbott was coming for and knew that if anything were found it would mean a long stretch.” He smoothed the back of his head and watched the steam hissing from the kettle, while Janet stood unheeding. Only when the lid began to jump about did she look away from Roger and make the tea.

“Let's go into the lounge,” suggested Mark.

They went in, and when they were sitting around, Roger said:

“Pep was upstairs, presumably.”

“It seems likely,” admitted Mark.

“He wanted you to create a din while he got in upstairs and he—” Roger paused, boggling at the actual words.

“Took something away!” exploded Janet.

“We're talking on supposition,” Mark said. “But if Pep learned that something incriminating was to be planted on you, obviously someone was to do it. There's your problem—who and why?”

“Yes.” Roger finished his tea in silence, then leaned back and studied the ceiling. The others did not interrupt his train of thought but Mark pretended to find some interest in a magazine. Suddenly Roger jumped to his feet, and stepped to the telephone in the corner of the room. After a short wait he said:

“Is Sir Guy Chatworth in, please?”

Janet stayed by the door, tensely. He was asked his name and then to hold on; he waited for a long time before Chatworth's servant—he had called the A.C. at his private flat, in Victoria—said that he was sorry but Sir Guy was not in and would not be in all the evening.

"So he won't talk to his favorite officer?" Mark said.

"It's fantastic!" exclaimed Janet. "I thought Chatworth was a friend. Roger, they can't believe that you've done anything to deserve this. I mean—if they do they're not worth a damn."

"Indignant female expresses herself forcefully," murmured Mark. "This is a conspiracy of silence. They wouldn't have acted this way and certainly wouldn't have put Abbott on the job if they hadn't meant to make it as hot as they could, so they must have a very good reason. It's no use blinking at facts, is it?"

"No," conceded Roger, glumly, and that ended the conversation for some minutes.

"I suppose I should start getting supper," said Janet, jumping up. "I won't be long."

She came back half an hour later with ham, cheese, bread, butter and a bowl of fruit. They finished supper and began the waiting game again.

They heard the gate open suddenly. Roger reached the front door before anyone knocked.

"Pep!" he exclaimed.

As soon as the door was closed again Roger switched on the light and looked at the smiling face of Morgan. A shiny man from his thin grey hair to his polished shoes—bright enough to see his face in, Morgan boasted proudly. In a good light, he scintillated. His cheeks shone like a new apple, his bright eyes gleamed, his astonishingly white teeth behind a full mouth seemed to sparkle. He was a chunky man, well-dressed but running to fat about the waist.

"*Hal*-lo, Handsome!" He patted Roger's elbow. "This is a fine old how-d'ye-do, isn't it?"

"Come in, Pep." Roger led him into the lounge, where he shook hands ceremoniously with Janet and smiled at Mark.

"You did your stuff very well, Mr. Lessing! I was upstairs, and believe me I thought you would have the police on you for disturbing the peace." He looked back at Roger and his smile grew strained. "Handsome, you won't take me wrong, I know, but I'm staking my reputation on you."

Janet and Mark seemed to fade into the background. Roger smiled, grimly, and asked:

"How are you doing that, Pep?"

"It's a remarkable business, it really is. You've guessed I came here when Abbott was on the spot, and removed a little trifle from upstairs?"

"We guessed," said Roger heavily.

"The little trifle was one thousand pounds," said Morgan, softly. "One thousand of the very best in five-pound notes, that is what I found upstairs underneath your wardrobe, Handsome. Look!" Pep took out his wallet and extracted two clean five-pound Bank of England notes. "I've brought two of them. I thought I'd better not bring them all in case Martin saw me come in and wanted to know what I was doing—he *might* have insisted on searching me." Morgan was nervous, but perky with it. "I don't know who's got their knife into you, but someone wants to put you on the spot."

Roger stared at him.

"You must feel pretty bad about it," said Morgan, "and so do I, Handsome. When I heard what was coming to you I came to the conclusion that it was a fix, and I couldn't let you down. Lucky thing you've got some friends at the Yard."

Roger said slowly: "What do you mean?"

"It was like this," said Morgan, moving to the table and sitting on the corner. "No names, no pack drill, but I was chatting with one of the women at the Yard and she started to talk about you. Some of the ladies get a proper crush on him, Mrs. West!" Morgan shot a sly glance at Janet. "She didn't exactly *tell* me, but she did say she had a nasty job on this afternoon, and she rambled on a bit—talked about having been told there would be some dough in the bedroom of a Yard man some time after lunch and it would be curtains for him if it was found. She didn't *say* you were the man concerned, but she'd been talking about you and she gave me a wink—kind of telling me to put two and two together. So I rang up Mr. Lessing and came along here and did my stuff."

After a long pause, Roger said:

"And you found a thousand pounds in notes?"

"Two hundred five-quid notes as sure as my name is Pep Morgan," declared Morgan. "I don't mind admitting I was pretty scared; if they'd found that dough on me they might have asked a lot of awkward questions. So I tied it up and registered it to *Post Restante*, Lower Strand, addressed to a Mr. North. I thought that sounded better than 'Smith,'" added Morgan, anxiously. "It's a bit close to West. I hope I didn't slip up there."

"No, you didn't slip up," said Roger, smiling into the little man's eyes. "Pep, I don't know how to begin to thank you."

"Oh, forget it. You've done me many a good turn, and I knew if they found that dough here you would have a taste of what you dish out to others, but *I* don't believe you would take bribes." He took out his cigarette-case but Janet stepped forward with a box. "Oh, ta," he said. "Bit of a shock for you, Mrs. West, I expect."

"It certainly wasn't a pleasure."

"I'll say it wasn't! Well, I've told you all I know, Handsome. I needn't say I know you won't let me down." He laughed and drew on his cigarette. "What a business it is, isn't it?"

"Did Winnie Marchant tip you off?"

Morgan wrinkled his forehead and repeated:

"No names, no pack drill. Was she here?"

Roger smiled.

"Yes. She gave Janet a piece of her mind!"

Morgan slid from the table and stood up, frowning, barely reaching Roger's chin.

"Handsome, what's it about?" he asked. "Who'd do the dirty on you like this?"

"I simply don't know," said Roger.

"You must have some idea," protested Morgan.

"One day I will have," Roger said softly. "I hope it won't be long. Will you take a commission from me, Pep?"

Morgan's little eyes glistened.

"I never thought I'd come to the day when a Chief Inspector would ask me that. Sure, sure. It's all in the way of business, there's no need for anyone to know how I came into it. You could have phoned me and asked me to try to find out whether anyone's trying to put you on the spot. It would be a natural thing to do. What's happened? Been suspended?"

"Not yet," said Roger.

"Nothing to prevent you from looking around yourself, then," observed Morgan. "And Mr. Lessing would lend a hand, as well as me. These fivers might help. Inspector West works from home, so to speak!" He laughed, quite gaily. "What do you want me to do for a start?"

"Make general inquiries, and try to find out whether anyone has a grudge against me. I suppose someone who's just come out of stir might be behind it."

"I thought of that," said Morgan. "But it would have to be a big shot—I mean, a thousand quid isn't chickenfeed. I've been thinking about those who've come out in the last month, and I don't know of anyone who could lay his hands on a thousand. Still, I don't mind trying, Handsome. There won't be any secret about it, will there?"

"None at all."

"Okay, then, I'm hired!" Morgan beamed, looked positively embarrassed when Janet came forward and kissed his cheeks. "He'd do the same for me," he mumbled and hurried to the door.

Roger watched him disappear into the gloom, and followed. It was not quite dark, and he could make out Morgan's shadowy figure. Suddenly he saw two others converge on the little man, and heard Detective Sergeant Martin:

"I want a word with you, Morgan."

Morgan protested in a high-pitched squeak. Roger drew nearer.

4

Information from Eddie

Perhaps because he thought that Roger would be following, Morgan held his ground and complained at being frightened out of his wits. He talked to Tiny Martin and the other policeman luridly enough to cheer Roger as he drew nearer, keeping against the hedges of the small gardens of Bell Street so that he would not be noticeable if Martin looked round. Ten feet away, he stood still.

"There's no need for you to behave like that," growled Martin. "You've co-operated with us before, haven't you?"

"I haven't had anyone run out on me like that. What do you want?"

"Superintendent Abbott would like a word with you."

"Well, he knows where I live. He seems to have gone off his rocker. So do you, Tiny." Although still aggrieved he sounded mollified, a sensible reaction to "Superintendent Abbott would *like* a word with you." "I've just been along to see Handsome West. You must be daft if you think he's crooked."

"Never mind that," said Martin.

He led the way towards King's Road. Roger stayed on the other side until a bus lumbered out of the gloom, stopped for the two men and went lurching onwards. Roger turned back to Bell Street. The other Yard man was still near the house and Roger caught a glimpse of him across the road.

Roger went into the house but did not return to the lounge. He took his raincoat out of a corner cupboard.

"What are you doing?" Janet asked.

"I'm going to the Yard," Roger said.

"Do you think—" began Janet.

"Is it wise?" asked Mark, outlined against the light of the lounge.

"I'm not suspended yet," said Roger. "I might pick up a hint from someone. If Winnie Marchant was prepared to let Pep know, one of the others might give me a hint of what it's all about." He put his hands on Janet's shoulders and kissed her. "I don't expect I'll be late," he said. "Make Mark play backgammon with you."

There were tears in Janet's eyes.

Roger went out, and paused on the porch to light a cigarette.

The plainclothes man was near the gate.

Roger drew on his cigarette so that his features were illuminated, then shone his torch into the other's face.

"I hope it keeps fine for you," said Roger. He was ridiculously glad that it was raining and cold enough to make the vigil an ordeal.

He did not get his car out, but walked briskly once he had grown accustomed to the gloom. He kept his eyes open for a taxi but had reached Sloane Square before he saw one. He was not sure that the Yard man had kept up with him, but thought it likely.

As he waited on the curb while the taxi turned in the road, footsteps, soft and stealthy, drew near him. He took it for granted that this was the plainclothes man and took no notice. The taxi pulled up and the driver expressed himself tersely on the weather.

"You going far?"

"Scotland Yard," said Roger. The shadowy figure behind him drew nearer and he wondered what the man was thinking. As he was climbing into the cab, the figure moved forward and a soft voice, certainly not belonging to the detective, broke the stillness.

"Excuse me, sir."

Roger turned his head, when half-in and half-out of the cab.

"Yes?" He was in no mood for casual encounters.

"I hope you won't think this an impertinence," said the stranger, "but I am most anxious to get to Piccadilly and the buses appear to have stopped running. I wonder if you would mind if I shared your cab?"

"What abaht askin' *me?*" demanded the driver.

"Oh, yes, indeed—if your fare wouldn't mind." The man looked towards the cabby. Roger noticed that he wore a trilby hat pulled low and had his coat collar turned up. As he saw the pale blur of his face he thought, impatiently, that it could not have happened at a worse time, but he said:

"Of course," and hoped that he sounded cordial.

There was no sign of anyone else nearby.

"Thank you so much," said the stranger, eagerly.

" 'Op in," said the driver.

Roger shifted to the far corner and the newcomer sat back with a sigh. He murmured that taxi-drivers were getting far too independent, it was most embarrassing to ask favors of them; it was very good indeed of Roger to allow him to share the taxi. *Had* he overheard him say that he was going to Scotland Yard?

That was an invitation to confide, but Roger made an evasive remark and sat back. The other continued to talk of the weather, the cold war situation, the possibility of the bank rate going up, the price of houses and income tax. Roger made an occasional comment.

The cab drew up outside the gates of Scotland Yard, and the cabby opened the glass partition.

"Needn't take you right in, need I?"

"No, this will do fine," said Roger.

He got out, stumbling over the other man's outstretched legs. He paid off the driver and watched the rear light fading into the night. He heard the footsteps of the policeman on duty and, a moment later, a bull's eye lantern was switched on.

"Is that necessary?"

"Oh—sorry, sir," said the policeman, putting the light out hastily. "Nasty night, sir, isn't it?"

"Bloody," growled Roger and strode towards the steps. It was some consolation to know that the man had no instructions to stop him. He went up the steps and into the hall, where a sergeant on duty saluted. He was an oldish fellow with a wisp of yellow hair and very thin features. It might have been the light and shade of the hall, but to Roger he seemed surprised as he said "Good evening."

" 'Evening, Bates," grunted Roger.

He passed no one downstairs nor on the stairs, but the walls themselves seemed cold and hostile. He had never been in the Yard before without feeling a certain friendliness in its atmosphere. He began to realize how much the place meant to him. The dimly-lighted passages, shadowy now, seemed to hold a menace which was no less disturbing because it was unwarranted.

He opened the door of his office quickly and stepped inside.

Eddie Day was sitting at his desk with a watchmaker's glass screwed to one of his prominent eyes. He looked up—and the glass dropped out, bounced from his desk and rolled along the floor.

Roger repressed a comment, loosened his coat and approached Day, looking down at the startled man.

"So you've heard, have you?"

"H-h-heard w-w-what?" stammered Eddie.

"Why pretend that you haven't, Eddie? Is it all round the Yard?"

Eddie closed his mouth, then bent down to retrieve the glass. His face was scarlet when he straightened up. Then he burst out:

"I've heard a rumor, yes!" To his credit he stopped pretending and did not try to make light of it. "You could have knocked me down with a feather. I don't know what to make of it, I really don't. You're the *last* one I would have thought—" he broke off. "What are you doing here? You've been suspended from duty, haven't you?"

"I haven't been told so."

"Oh, well, perhaps that's a rumor," Eddie said hopefully. "I hope it is, Handsome. I can't believe—" he paused and then went on: "Did Abbott have a search-warrant?"

"He did. And he used it."

"Blimey!" Eddie pushed his lips forward and eyed Roger owlishly. "I just couldn't believe it when I heard. When Bennett told me I thought he was joking, but he said he'd seen the warrant. What's the Old Man got to say?"

Roger said: "The Assistant Commissioner hasn't thought it worth discussing with me."

"Strewth!" exclaimed Eddie.

"Eddie, do something for me," said Roger softly. "If you know what they think I've been doing, if you've any idea from where they got the tip, tell me. I was pretty sharp with Abbott, because I know nothing about it. What do you know?"

"Handsome, I'm with you. I think it's all a lot of nonsense. I can't understand the Old Man. All I know is that you're supposed to have accepted bribes over a period of the last three months."

"From whom?" Roger demanded.

"The squeak came from Joe Leech."

"Oh," said Roger. He stepped restlessly to the fireplace, where the fire glowed red. He knew "Joe Leech," a bookmaker in the East End who kept within the law and was allowed to go to the extreme limits because he was a regular source of information to the police. His information was usually reliable and the police were often obliged to act on it. Few at the Yard had any liking for Leech, whose bad reputation in the East End was well known. Two or three times a year he had to be given police protection after he had squealed and friends of his victims had threatened violence. One thing was certain. Leech would not have done this unless he believed the allegation to be true or unless he had been heavily bribed.

"Don't say I told you," pleaded Eddie.

He heard someone approaching and put his glass hastily to his eye. The footsteps passed. Eddie stared at Roger with his glass at his eye, his forehead and nose wrinkled.

"It's a bad do, Handsome, no doubt about that."

He broke off when the telephone on his desk rang. He answered it and Roger judged, from his manner, that it was Chatworth. Eddie was more impressed by the Assistant Commissioner than most Chief Inspectors, although Chatworth had a reputation for being a martinet.

Eddie replaced the receiver and stood up, gathering some papers from his untidy desk.

"Got to go and see the Old Man," he said, in a confidential undertone. "He wants my report on those dud notes. You know the ones I mean."

"Yes," said Roger, with a flicker of interest. "Are they slush?" He thought of the £1,000 now at the Strand Post office waiting for "Mr. North" but it was too early to ask Eddie's opinion of the two specimens; Eddie was not a man to be trusted too far in these circumstances. There were two Yard men who might take the risk of helping him, but one, Sloan, was on holiday.

"Stake my reputation on it," said Eddie, half-way to the door. "They're good, though. Er—best of luck, Handsome. If I can do anything let me know."

Alone in the office, Roger looked about him, putting his hand in his raincoat pockets. He felt an envelope in there but thought nothing of it. The green-distempered walls displayed a few photographs, including one, old and faded, of a Suffragette procession down Whitehall in 1913, two cricket XI's, one of them including himself, two or three maps of London districts and several calendars. On one of the desks was a small vase of fading daffodils. The fireplace was littered with cigarette ends and the carpet, with several threadbare patches, had a few trodden into it. The desks were bright yellow but, in places, the polish had worn off and the bare wood showed. There were little partitions for different papers—*"For Attention"*—*"For Review"*—*"Mail In."* Suddenly he stopped reading the black, stencilled letters, for his own desk was empty; everything had been removed since he had been there that morning.

He turned away, taking his hand out of his pocket and drawing the envelope with it. He looked down at the crumpled paper, frowning. It was thick and newish-looking; had it been in his pocket for some time it would have been grubby. He remembered thinking that morning that it was a fortnight since he had last worn his raincoat.

It was sealed and there was no writing on it.

He inserted a finger at one end and ripped it open. Inside was a single slip of paper on which were two or three lines of block letter writing, upside down. He turned it swiftly and read:

> Dear West,
>
> I've another proposition I think will interest you. It will pay even better than the last. Meet me at the usual place, tomorrow, Wednesday, at 7.30, will you?
>
> K.

At first startled, then tight-lipped, Roger re-read it. All that it meant and all it might have led to passed through his mind, together with a fact which he had to face and which almost stupefied him. *"Another proposition,"* inferring that there had been plenty of others; *"It will pay even better."* ". . . meet me at the usual place . . ."

A film of sweat broke out on his forehead.

To Abbott it would be just the evidence he wanted, and he had brought it into the Yard himself! He might easily have left his coat on a peg and gone to try to see Chatworth, which was his chief reason for coming. He stared down, studying the "K" more closely; it was a carefully-formed letter; the whole note had been written by someone expert in using a pen. It was in drawing-ink, jet black and vivid against the white paper.

He screwed it up, with the envelope, turned, and placed it carefully in the middle of the glowing embers of the fire. It began to scorch but took a long time to blaze up. He heard someone approaching and turned with his back to the fire. As he did so the paper caught alight, making a flame bright enough to cast his shadow on the nearest desk. If someone came in and saw it they might try to retrieve the evidence.

The man outside passed, footsteps ringing on the cement floor. Roger stirred the blazing paper with his toe. In a few seconds it was just black ash, glowing red in places and giving off a few sparks which were quickly drawn up the chimney. He went to an easy chair to recover from the shock and to face the obvious fact; the envelope had been put in his pocket either at his own house or in the taxi.

5

No Welcome for Roger

No one came to the office.

Roger sat in an armchair of faded green hide. Nothing seemed quite real and the appearance of the note in his pocket seemed fantastic. He could remember every word and every characteristic of the lettering, the quality of the white paper and its thickness. He half wished he still had it, but it must have been too dangerous to keep.

Abbott must have searched the raincoat, so the note had not been there at five o'clock. No one had been in Bell Street except his friends and the police. The thought that Morgan might have put it there could be dismissed at once. The more he considered it the more convinced he was that the soft-voiced man of the taxi had inserted it when Roger had got out of the cab.

Roger stood up, and went to the door.

Chatworth's office was on the next floor. Roger walked to the stairs and met two Detective Inspectors coming down. They looked surprised to see him. Along Chatworth's corridor a door opened and Superintendent Bliss, broad and fat and with a voice like a dove, almost knocked into him.

"West!" he exclaimed.

"Bliss?" said Roger.

"Eh—didn't expect to see you," said Bliss and hurried off. Two men in the office stared at Roger as if at something strange. Tight-lipped, Roger went on to Chatworth's office. There was a light under the door and he could hear Eddie Day's sing-song voice. At the best of times it was unwise to interrupt Chatworth; he would have to wait.

Two corridors away was a common-room, for higher officials. It had a billiard table, table tennis, darts and all the paraphernalia of a club. Nearing the door Roger could hear the murmur of voices, and bursts of laughter. He went in and walked across the room without drawing attention to himself. Someone looked up from the billiard table and he heard his name uttered *sotto voce*. Two other men turned to stare. Others, by the walls playing chess and draughts, two card parties and table-tennis players, all stopped just long enough for the pause to register.

He felt the blood flooding his cheeks.

No one spoke to him and he made no attempt to start a conversation. Fair-haired, youthful Inspector Cornish, who had recently been promoted from one of the Divisions, was the nearest approach to a close friend Roger had at the Yard. He was the only one here who might risk helping him.

Cornish looked up from an evening paper, colored and averted his eyes. Roger turned on his heel. He was by the door when he heard his name called and, looking over his shoulder, saw Cornish hurrying towards him, his fresh face alive with concern.

"Handsome, do you know what's being said?"

"And believed, apparently," rejoined Roger.

"*Is* there any truth in it?" Cornish demanded.

"You ought to know better than to ask," Roger said. "It's a *canard* and will be recognized as such one day. Then what will all my good friends say when they come begging *Superintendent* West for favors?" He looked contemptuously round the room and felt suddenly unaffected by the hostility and the strength of the feeling against him. He would have felt strongly towards anyone whom he believed to have committed a cardinal crime in a policeman's calendar. They had no time or sympathy for a renegade. He went on, sounding almost light-hearted. "You'd better be careful, Corny, or you'll be looked upon as an accessory! Good night!"

He went out, hearing the hum of conversation which followed. The door opened again and Cornish hurried after him.

"Roger. *Roger!*" The other was distressed and Roger turned and waited. "Look here, old man," said Cornish, "just answer me this—*did* you do it?"

"I did not."

"Is there anything I can do?" asked Cornish abruptly.

Roger warmed towards him.

"If you really want to stick your neck out you can try to find out the name and address of the taxi-driver who picked me up at Sloane Square about three-quarters of an hour ago and dropped me here. I shared the cab with a man going on to Piccadilly." That was as much as he dared ask.

"How will it help?" Cornish demanded.

"I'm not going to let you get involved with details," Roger said. "If you can find out just the cabby's name and address, it could help a lot. Don't take this too hard," he added, cheerfully, "it won't last for ever!"

He went on his way, grateful to Cornish, and was smiling to himself when he turned the corner. Sir Guy Chatworth, a large, burly man wearing a long mackintosh which rustled about his legs, and a wide-brimmed hat, nearly but not quite a Stetson, was shutting his office door. His large, round features were set in a scowl, by no means unusual. His natural color was brick red.

"Good evening, sir," said Roger.

Chatworth raised his massive head and stared at him. He put the key in his pocket, and demanded heavily:

"What do you imagine you are doing here?"

"I've come for two things," Roger said. "First, an interview with you, sir, and second, to apply for a release from duty for four weeks."

"Oh," said Chatworth, ominously. "You want release from duty, do you? Well, you can't have it. You are suspended from duty."

"That's news to me," said Roger. "I've had no notification, sir."

Chatworth thrust his chin forward, narrowed his eyes, often round and deceptively wondering and innocent. "It isn't dated until tomorrow morning. You're being clever, are you, West? If you think you can apply for release and escape the stigma of suspension, you're wrong."

"I've been wrong about so many things that nothing will surprise me."

"What do you mean?" snapped Chatworth.

"I had always been under the impression that any man of yours would receive scrupulously fair treatment," Roger said. "It was a nasty shock to find I was wrong about that."

"You had your opportunity to discuss this with me," Chatworth said. He stood by the door, feet planted wide apart, his mackintosh draped about him like a night-shirt which was too large. He pushed back the big hat and revealed his high forehead and the front of his bald head. At the sides was a thick fringe of close curls, blond turning grey.

"I had no such thing," said Roger.

"You appear to be forgetting yourself," Chatworth said coldly. "You were requested by Superintendent Abbott to come here to see me, and you refused. You were also insolent to a superior officer."

"In the same circumstances any man should be 'insolent' to an officer who invades the privacy of his home, adopts an arrogant and overbearing manner to his wife and tries to take advantage of seniority," Roger said clearly. "Superintendent Abbott appears to have misled you, sir. He did not say that you wished to see me. He asked me to go with him for questioning. As I knew nothing of the circumstances and he would not give me any information, I refused."

Chatworth frowned, then dug his hand into his pocket. He took out the key, unlocked the door and pushed it open, striding into the room ahead of Roger, who followed without an invitation.

"Close the door." Chatworth walked to his flat-topped desk. Everything in the room was modern, most of the furniture was of tubular steel, filing cabinets and desk were of polished metal which looked like glass. There was concealed wall-lighting and a single desk-lamp, all of which were controlled by a main switch.

Chatworth unbuttoned his mackintosh but did not take it off. He placed his hat on the desk in front of him and looked up at Roger, who was standing a yard from the desk without expression. Chatworth pushed his lips forward in deliberation, then said:

"I am grievously disappointed in you, West."

"And I in you, sir."

"Are you out of your senses?"

"It is a very grave matter for me, sir," Roger said. "I don't think it has been properly handled. If a sergeant dealt with a parallel case in the same way I should have his stripes."

He had burned his boats, but Chatworth would think no worse of him and it might enable him to force a hearing. He had won a minor triumph by getting into the room at all. He stood at ease, with one hand in his mackintosh pocket, and thought of the letter from "K."

Then Chatworth nearly floored him.

"Who broke into your house while Abbott was there?"

"I don't understand you, sir," Roger said.

"Yes you do. While Abbott was in your house Lessing arrived and drummed on the piano while a man broke in through a first floor window, and removed the evidence which Abbott went to find. Don't lie to me, West. You think that was clever, but it was a mistake."

"To my knowledge there was never any evidence in my house which would convict me of accepting bribes. I have never accepted a bribe in my life. I don't know where you got your information, nor how long I have been suspect, but I do know that I think the methods adopted to trap me are disgraceful. You appear to have prejudged me, you've denied me the right to enter a defense. My best course, I think, is to refer the matter to the Home Secretary."

"Are you trying to *frighten* me?"

"I am giving you notice of my intention," said Roger. "That's more than anyone did for me." He paused but Chatworth simply sat back and stared at him; the desk-lamp shone on his polished cranium.

Looking at a man who had often been friendly and with whom he had worked for several years, one whom he had almost regarded with hero-worship, Roger felt a quickening tension. Until then, he had thought it just possible that Chatworth had deliberately planned to smear him so that he could work surreptitiously. The last hope should have died when he had found "K's" note, which was proof of evil intent.

Now he saw the situation for what it was, absurd but highly dangerous. Chatworth was not an ogre, but a reasonable human beneath his gruff manner. Roger stepped forward and planted both hands on the desk.

"I know that you must have strong reasons for what you've done," he said. "You might at least give me the chance to answer the allegations. My record at the Yard should entitle me to that. The case must be more serious even than the seriousness of accepting bribes, or you wouldn't have been so arbitrary. And Abbott's visit doesn't make sense." He saw Chatworth going even redder. "If I were guilty, I wouldn't be fool enough to keep evidence in my house."

"That's enough, West," said Chatworth in a more reasonable tone. "Sit down." That was a ray of hope. So was the way Chatworth pushed a box of cigarettes towards him. He lit up, and Chatworth bit the end off a cheroot. "For the first time I'm beginning to think I might be wrong," Chatworth went on. "Why do you want four weeks' leave?"

"To investigate this affair for myself."

Chatworth unlocked a drawer in his desk and drew out a manila folder. Roger leaned back and drew on his cigarette. The office was quiet except for the rustling of papers, until Chatworth glanced up and said sharply: "How do you account for seven payments of two hundred and fifty pounds paid into your account at the Mid-Union Bank, Westminster, during the last three months? Cash payments, always in one-pound notes. Where did you get the money?"

Roger was stupefied. "It's not true!" he protested.

"Now, come. I have seen the account, talked to the cashier and the manager. Your wife made the payments."

"Nonsense!" said Roger.

"Are you telling me that you don't know what money there is in your account?"

"I use the Mid-Union Bank only for occasional transactions," Roger said. "It's a supplementary to my main account at Barclays, Chelsea. I've sent no credit to Mid-Union for at least six months. Nor has my wife."

Chatworth said:

"Look at that."

He handed a bank paying-in book across the desk. It was a small one, with half the pages torn out, leaving only the counterfoils. Roger saw that the first entries were in his handwriting—the book was undoubtedly his. He glanced through it, seeing a payment of fifty pounds which he had made in the September of the previous year. From then on—beginning in the middle of January—there were the payments which Chatworth had mentioned. The official stamp of the Mid-Union Bank with initials scrawled across it was there and the name at the top of each counterfoil was his.

Roger turned the counterfoils. The first shock over, he was able to study the writing and he noticed the regular lettering, it was almost copperplate writing, *such as the man who had signed himself "K" might have written.*

"Well?" demanded Chatworth.

"And my wife is supposed to have paid these in?" said Roger. "No, sir, it didn't happen that way. The money has been paid in, all right. They've taken a lot of trouble to frame me, haven't they?" He smiled, looked almost carefree. "I suppose someone representing herself to be my wife made the calls?"

"The description of the woman in every case is identifiable with your wife," Chatworth declared.

"The description of any attractive, average build dark-haired woman with a flair for dressing well would do for that."

"You seem remarkably pleased with yourself," said Chatworth, sarcastically.

"I'm greatly relieved, sir! This is obviously one of your main items of evidence. My wife didn't visit the bank and the bank's cashiers will say so when they see her. You'll arrange for several cashiers to see her, won't you?"

"Yes," said Chatworth. He leaned back and closed one eye. His pendulous jowl pressed against his collar, only half of which was visible. "You're *remarkably* smug," he remarked. "You could have sent another young woman."

Roger laughed. "Aren't you letting yourself be carried away, sir?"

"*What* did you say?"

"If I were to advance a theory like that, without evidence, you would tell me not to put myself out on a limb," Roger said. "Someone else paid that money into my account and whoever it was can be found. When she's found we'll have at least part of the answer to all this. May I ask what other evidence you have?"

Chatworth said in a strained voice: "West, are you a consummate liar or do you seriously suggest that you have been framed?"

"Obviously, I've been cleverly framed," said Roger. "You can't have any unanswerable evidence or you wouldn't have waited so long before acting. You can't charge me or you would have done by now. May I have that four weeks' leave of absence, sir?"

"I don't know," said Chatworth. "When did you arrange for Morgan to break into your house?"

With anyone else, Roger might have given himself away. For years he had been used to such unexpected questions and he had trained himself never to be taken off his guard. His mood changed, however, but he felt sure that Morgan would have made no admission, so he answered promptly:

"I didn't."

“Morgan’s finger-prints were found in your bedroom this afternoon and he was seen visiting you this evening.”

“There’s no reason why his prints shouldn’t be there,” Roger said. “He’s visited me often enough.”

“Do you usually take visitors to your bedroom?”

“Frequently,” Roger replied. “I use it as an office sometimes. Morgan has been helpful recently, and as soon as I realized what Abbott was after I asked him to help me.”

“Help you to do what?”

“Find the answer to this mystery.”

Chatworth closed one eye again and looked at the ceiling. His fingers, covered with a mat of fair hair, drummed on the polished surface of the desk and Roger waited with growing tension.

6

The Lady So Beautiful

"Go on," urged Mark Lessing.

"What did he say?" demanded Janet breathlessly.

"Not a great deal," said Roger, who had just finished telling them the story of his interview with Chatworth. "Apparently Pep's story bore mine out. The denial that Jan had been paying the cash in floored the old boy, I think. He was quite reasonable, as far as it goes. In the circumstances, suspension was the only thing, and leave of absence wouldn't do. He's right, of course. He gave me the impression that he expects me to get around a bit and will be prepared to listen to any evidence I dig up."

"So I should think!" exclaimed Janet. "I'll never like that man again."

"Oh, I don't know," said Roger. "Those entries, occasional rumors from Joe Leech"—he uttered the bookmaker's name very softly—"and other indications all pointing towards me, must have made it look black."

It was nearly midnight but none of them looked tired and there was a kettle singing on the hob and an empty teapot warming by the fire. Roger was sitting back in an easy chair wriggling his toes inside his slippers. Mark was opposite him, and Janet was curled up on a settee between the two armchairs.

"He didn't tell you who's supposed to have bribed you?" inquired Mark.

"No. He was reticent about that, which probably means that

he doesn't know for certain, but that he thinks the case hasn't really broken open yet. He didn't say much more," he repeated. "A few generalities suggested that this is supposed to have been going on since about Christmas, when I hit upon some particularly clever racket and accepted bribes and held my tongue. Abbott's been working on the case from the beginning."

"What a snake he is," said Janet.

"It wasn't a pleasant job," Roger replied, "and—"

"Darling, there are limits to the spirit of forgiveness."

"Oh, I don't know," interjected Mark. "Better too much than too little, and although no one loves Abbott, he's good at his particular brand of inquiry. When the cashiers have said 'no' about Janet we'll all feel better. You learned nothing else?"

"Not from Chatworth. Eddie Day gave me Joe Leech's name and Cornish promised to find the taxi-driver." He had told them about the note from "K." "If I can find out where the other passenger went it might help. The copperplate writing and the paper—I wish I'd kept the envelope but it was too risky!—the drawing-ink, Joe Leech and the woman who's paid the cash in, and those five-pound notes. With luck and hard going we'll get through. I wish I had some kind of idea why it's being done," went on Roger. "That's one of the things at which Chatworth boggles most. Why should there be a deliberate attempt to frame me? I've been over the possible revenge motives, but Pep's right. No one's come out of stir lately who would be rich enough to try it. In any case, it's too fantastic a notion."

The kettle began to boil and he leaned forward and poured water in the pot. There were some sandwiches on a tray and Mark bit into one.

"The reason why," he murmured. "That seems to be the first thing to discover, Roger. Shall I set my great mind to work?"

"Not yet, thanks!" said Roger, horrified. They laughed. "Your first job, if you'll do it, is to interview Joe Leech. Joe may be smart enough to outwit Pep."

Mark grinned. "For that oblique compliment, many thanks! Er—Roger."

"Yes?"

"One little thing you might have forgotten," Mark said, "and it could be significant. I mean, the attempt to involve Janet. The first assumption might be that it was just to strengthen the evidence against you, but it might also mean that the family is to be involved."

Roger frowned. "I can't think that's likely. Did I say that Chatworth is going to send Cornish with you to the Mid-Union tomorrow, Jan? I think he's afraid you will scratch Abbott's eyes out!"

He laughed, and the atmosphere, already very much easier, grew almost gay.

The tension at the house while Roger had been out had been almost unbearable. It had been broken only by a telephone call from Pep Morgan, who had reported his encounter with Tiny Martin and told Mark that he had gone to the Yard and been questioned. He had been asked whether he had been at Bell Street earlier in the day, as well as to the reason why he had gone that night. Pep had answered on similar lines to Roger and had been released with a somber warning from Abbott to "be careful."

They went to bed just after one o'clock and, surprisingly, Roger went to sleep quickly. Janet lay awake a long while, listening to his heavy breathing and to Mark snoring in the spare room.

Mark was up first and disturbed the others by whistling in his bath. They breakfasted soon after eight o'clock and, just after nine, Mark left for the East End. Roger was tempted to go with Janet to the Mid-Union Bank, but thought it wiser to wait at Chelsea. She left soon after ten o'clock, met Cornish at Piccadilly and received the paying-in book from him and, at the small branch of the provincial bank made out a credit entry for fifty pounds, in cash, which Roger had taken out of his safe.

Cornish was nowhere in sight when she paid it in.

In spite of all the circumstances and her knowledge that she had never been inside the bank before, she felt on edge. The cashier was a middle-aged man with beetling brows; there was something sinister about him, about the tapping of a typewriter behind a partition and the cold austerity of the little bank itself. The cashier peered at her over the tops of steel-rimmed spectacles, counted the notes carefully, stamped the book and handed it back to her.

"Good morning, madam," he said.

"Good morning," gasped Janet and hurried out, feeling stifled.

She did not see Cornish immediately, but went by arrangement to the Regent Palace Hotel. She sat in the coffee lounge, and waited on tenterhooks. After twenty minutes Cornish came hurrying in, smiling cheerfully. Her spirits rose.

"Hallo, Mrs. West!" Cornish reached her, his smile widening. "You'll be glad to hear that he has never seen you before!"

Janet drew a deep breath.

"Thank heavens for that! I was half afraid that—" she broke off and forced a laugh. "But I mustn't be absurd!"

"I've telephoned the Yard, so that's all right," Cornish said. "You'll have some coffee, won't you?"

"I must let Roger know first. I'll phone from here."

"Thank God for that," Roger said over the telephone. "I was half-afraid that the cashier would go crazy."

"So was I," said Janet. "I suppose we'll imagine idiotic things everywhere until all this is over. I must go, darling, Cornish is being very sweet. He's getting some coffee."

"Remind him to find that cabby's address," Roger said.

Greatly relieved, he stepped from the telephone to the window and looked out into Bell Street. One of Abbott's men was still on duty there. He felt like laughing at him, much happier now that he had a chance to fight back. Once the initial suspicion was gone, the whole organization of the Yard would support him.

He hummed to himself as he lit a cigarette and then, frowning slightly, saw a powerful limousine drawing up outside the house. The driver glanced about him as if looking for the name of a house before pulling up opposite Roger's.

Abbott's man, betraying no interest, strolled along the opposite pavement.

A chauffeur climbed down from the car and opened the rear door. There was a pause before a woman stepped out. She was extremely attractive, and beautifully turned out in a black and white suit trimmed with mink.

Through the open window, Roger heard her say:

"I will go, Bott."

Her voice was husky, the sun glistened on her teeth. She walked up the narrow path while the chauffeur stood at attention by the gate. As she disappeared from Roger's sight, the front door-bell rang.

Before Roger went into the hall he smoothed his hair down and straightened his tie. When he opened the door he was smiling. It wasn't difficult to smile at a woman as attractive as this stranger.

"Good morning," he said.

"Is Mrs. West in, please?"

"I'm afraid not," said Roger. "I'm her husband."

The woman said as if surprised: "You are Chief Inspector West?"

"Yes. Will you come in?"

She hesitated and then said:

"I really wanted to see Mrs. West."

When he stepped aside, she entered the hall and he showed her into the front room. She moved very gracefully. Disarmed at first, Roger grew wary as she loosened the jacket, smiled, and sat down in Janet's chair. "Will you please tell your wife I called?" she asked.

"Yes," said Roger. "Whom shall I say?"

"Mrs. Cartier," replied the woman, taking a card from her bag. "Mr. West, I wonder if you will give me *your* support? It is such a good cause and I was told that Mrs. West would probably be invaluable to us."

"Us?" queried Roger, who had not looked at her card.

"To the Society," said Mrs. Cartier.

Roger glanced at the card, which was engraved: "*Mrs. Sylvester Cartier, President, the Society of European Relief, Welbeck Street, W.1.*" He had heard of the Society which, when it had first been formed, had been visited by Yard officials to make sure of its *bona fides.* He remembered that it was registered as a Refugee Charity and that its patrons included some of the most distinguished names in *Who's Who.*

Janet worked for several welfare societies, and he assumed that Mrs. Cartier had obtained her name from one of them. Yet he could not help feeling that her visit on this particular morning was a remarkable coincidence. He remembered that Janet had said that they would be reading sinister qualities in the most innocent matters; this was probably an example.

"How can my wife help you?" he inquired.

"Her enthusiasm and organizing ability are so well known," said Mrs. Sylvester Cartier. "I have been told that she is quite exceptional. You know of our Charity, of course?"

"I've heard of it."

"Then you will help to persuade her?"

Roger said: "I think I should know more of what you want her to do."

"But that is so difficult to explain precisely," Mrs. Cartier said. "There is a great deal of work. Our Society will make strenuous efforts to assist the professional people among the refugees—who so often cannot be helped by the United Nations or other official organizations, Mr. West. So many groups cater for the common man, but the professional classes need help just as badly. They must be rehabilitated"—she pronounced that word carefully, as if she had rehearsed frequently and yet was not really sure of it—"and enabled to contribute towards their adopted nations. I will not weary you with details, but please do ask your wife to consider my appeal for her services most sympathetically. I am at the office most afternoons between two and four o'clock." She rose and smiled as she extended her gloved hand. "I won't keep you longer, Mr. West. Thank you so much."

"Good-bye," said Roger, formally.

Janet would have accused him of being in a daze as he saw her out and watched her get into the car; a Daimler. The chauffeur tucked the rug about her, closed the door and went round to his seat. The car purred off, revealing the Yard man on the other side of the road.

"Well, well," said Roger. "I wonder what Janet will say?"

It was just after eleven and he did not expect Janet back until after twelve. He leaned back in his chair and tried to concentrate on his immediate problem.

The payments to his account at the Mid-Union Bank had started in mid-January. From that time someone had decided to try to destroy his reputation and, at best, to get him drummed out of the Yard. He had dismissed the possibility that it was revenge, but there must be some reason and he could imagine only that, about four months earlier, he had made some discovery which, if he followed it up, would have startling results.

"Some unwitting discovery," he mused. "Something which made me more dangerous than a policeman would normally be."

He began to go back over his activities in December. He had finished off three minor cases of burglary, one of forgery with Eddie Day's help, one sordid murder case. He had made some inquiries into aliens living in England and whose activities were suspect. These aliens had succeeded in proving their good behavior. Aliens—

He sat up abruptly. *Aliens* and the Society of European Relief! What a fool he had been not to see that connection before! Mrs. Cartier might be English by marriage but she had almost certainly been born an alien. Others connected with the Society might be as well, one of his inquiries might have touched upon the Society. In sudden excitement he began to trace back again, trying to remember every visit he had made, every name which had been suspect. "Cartier" was not among them, yet even that held a French ring.

Yet would the woman have come and risked setting up such a

train of thought? If the mystery concerned the Society, she would surely realize that it might start him thinking, and she might even know of his plight.

He went to the writing desk and began to make out a list of names, stopping only when his memory failed him. He grew so absorbed that even when Janet had not returned by one o'clock, he did not pause to wonder why she was so late. Nor did he wonder what progress Mark was making.

7

The Fears of Joe Leech

Mark Lessing strode along the Street of Ninety-Nine Bridges, not far from London Bridge. He was a noticeable figure in that part of London. He seemed oblivious of the dirt, the smells from small shops and markets, the grime which floated from the river and the spectral outlines of warehouses. Now and again he passed rows of hovels, some of them with the doors and windows open, most of them tightly closed and looking forlorn. Tugs hooted mournfully on the river. Covered gangways connecting one warehouse with another crossed the narrow street at intervals. Quays and locks, crossed by revolving bridges, were crossed with depressing frequency. Now and again he looked over the side of a bridge and saw the green slime undisturbed for many months. Yet there was a great hustle of activity, many voices were raised, horses and lorries passed along the cobbles in what seemed an endless stream.

Mark reached Rose Street, a narrow turning off the Street of Ninety-Nine Bridges. Its houses were squat and ugly, but halfway along were two larger buildings, one a school, the other a public house. The latter, called for some incalculable reason the "Saucy Sue," was a grey-faced, grim-looking Victorian edifice with its windows boarded up.

Joe Leech owned the "Saucy Sue."

He did not work in the bar, although he did the buying and handled all the business with the breweries. He had a manager, a bald-headed, lantern-jawed individual named Clay, whose face was exactly the color of clay and whose features had a trick of immobility which made them appear fashioned out of the same material. Clay was reputed to be the most saturnine man in the East End of London and it was said that he was the only man who had worked for Joe Leech for more than six months.

The "Saucy Sue" was not open to the public when Mark reached it, just after ten o'clock, but the front door was open and a young girl, with bright fair hair, was scrubbing the doorsteps.

When he drew nearer Mark saw that she was older than he had thought, but painfully thin. When she became aware of his shadow, she looked up and brushed the hair back from her eyes. She had a smudge of dirt on the side of her nose but the rest of her face was scrubbed clean and looked rosy. Her round bright eyes regarded him with guarded curiosity.

"Hallo," said Mark.

"Watcher want?" demanded the girl.

"Is Mr. Leech in?"

"I dunno."

"Oh, come," protested Mark. "You must know."

"I said I dunno an' I means I dunno," said the girl. "If yer wants ter know anyfink, wot's the matter wiv' going inside?" She pointed towards the open door and then dipped her work-grimed hand into the water. Mark shrugged his shoulders and stepped over the threshold.

A man behind the bar was polishing glasses. Behind him the brasses of the taps and the faucets at the end of the wine and spirit bottles glistened in spite of the gloomy interior. The floor was strewn with clean saw-dust. This man was Clay.

"Watcher want Mr. Leech for?" he demanded.

"Is he in?" asked Mark.

"You ain't answered my question."

"I want to see Leech. Tell him so and be quick about it."

"Can't see Mr. Leech wivvout a good reason," Clay said stubbornly.

“I have a good reason.”

“If yer ’ave, wot is it?”

The harsh, monotonous sound of scrubbing came from another room. Clay continued to stare, but finally admitted defeat, opening his lips but closing them again before he demanded grudgingly:

“What’s yer name?”

“Lessing. Mark Lessing. I want to see Leech on important business.”

Clay turned and walked stiffly to a closed door and pushed through it. Outside, feminine voices were raised, and Mark grinned when he heard a woman say:

“Got a toff to see yer, duck?”

“Wot, me see *’im?*” demanded the girl with the pail.

Mark lit a cigarette, felt uneasy when Clay did not return after five minutes, then heard more footsteps on the pavement. A quavering voice, that of an old man, demanded:

“You open yet, Lizzie?”

“Go and hide yerself!” ordered Lizzie. “What’s the use o’ worritting me every morning? You won’t git a drink until twelve o’clock. Git out’ve my way.”

“Now, Lizzie,” remonstrated the man with the quavering voice, “I was only arsking a civil question wot wants a civil answer.” He lowered his voice. “Seen the Masher arahnd?”

“No, I ain’t!”

“If I could see Joe I could tell ’im a thing or two,” declared the ancient. “If ’e knew what I knew he wouldn’t mind lettin’ me ’ave one.” Mark heard Lizzie’s unprintable retort, followed by the shuffling footsteps of the old man. He stepped to the door. Ten yards along the street the man was walking slowly, sliding his feet along the pavement. The heels of his boots were worn down to the uppers, his trousers were ragged and patches were coming away from the stitches. His shirt was filthy. He wore a pair of braces, the back tongues pinned to the top of his trousers. He turned into a little house twenty yards further on. Mark watched him thoughtfully and was startled by Clay’s voice.

"Leech ain't in," Clay announced. "It's no use."

"Are you quite sure?"

"I said so, didn't I?"

Mark took two half-crowns from his pocket and held them on the palm of his hand.

"If yer was to offer me a fiver I couldn't tell yer where he is. 'E ain't in—you clear out."

One of the remarkable things about Joe Leech was the fact that normally he made himself available to any caller. A good purveyor of inside information had to be catholic in his friends, and Mark knew his reputation. As well as being the owner of the "Saucy Sue" and a bookmaker, he was a "commission agent." He handled all kinds of strange commodities and took commission on an astonishing variety of transactions. The only times when he was unapproachable were during periods when he had squealed to the police and vengeful criminals were out for his blood. His philosophy of life was that anger burned out, and if one kept out of the way for a few days trouble would blow over. Then Joe Leech, short, plump, and gaudily-dressed, would decorate the drab streets again.

"Clay, you lie too easily," said Mark, sorrowfully. He pushed past and reached the door. Clay swore and jumped at him, but Mark slipped through the doorway and hurried up the narrow wooden stairs. The house smelled of beer and decaying vegetables. There was a narrow landing with three closed doors and he wondered which of them was Joe Leech's.

". . . murder yer!" Clay was bellowing.

Mark opened one door of a bedroom, the bed unmade. He closed it and opened a second door as Clay reached the top of the stairs and he stopped there breathing vengeance. Mark looked into a long, narrow room. It was a parlor filled with cheap modern furniture and with wallpaper so gaudy that it was an offense to the eye.

Sitting at a table at the far end of the room was Joe Leech, a vision in puce pajamas, with tousled hair, bloodshot eyes and sagging cheeks. There were two curious things about Joe; the visible one was his small, cupid's mouth, soft and womanish; the audible one his pure tenor voice, not childish yet certainly not manly. He was proud of being self-educated and affected a horror of the Cockney accent; his was a neutral one and usually he managed most of his aspirates.

Mark left the door open and stepped towards the man, who had a table-drawer open, pushed against his stomach, and his right hand hidden inside the drawer.

"Why, Joe!" exclaimed Mark. "What's all the to-do about? I only want a word with you." Leech snatched his hand from the drawer and slammed it to; it caught at one side and gave Mark the opportunity of seeing an automatic. Then Joe slammed it home.

"Who are you and what do you want?"

"We've met before, Joe. What's frightening the wits out of you?"

Joe gulped. "I—I—I'm not frightened."

"I thought I recognized all the symptoms."

"If you don't sling your hook, mister, you won't recognize yer own dial," growled Clay from behind him. The manager had a poker gripped in his right hand, his stiff movements holding a menace which made Mark back hastily to the wall. "Clear out."

"Tell him to go away, Joe," said Mark.

Leech darted a sidelong glance towards him, and licked his lips. He stood up and rounded the table, putting a hand on Clay's arm.

"It's all right, it's all right, Clay, I recognize Mr. Lessing now." He smiled weakly. "I didn't know who it was at first, if I'd known it was Mr. Lessing I'd have told you to show him up right away. You know I would, Mr. Lessing, don't you?"

"Shut the door behind you, Clay." Mark waited until the door was closed, watching Joe's movement towards a corner cupboard, opening it and taking out glasses and a bottle. Joe's head jerked backwards as he drank. He turned round, a glass in one hand and a bottle of whisky in the other.

"Have a drink, Mr. Lessing? I was up all night, so it's just a nightcap for me. I was going to have forty winks just before you came. No peace for the wicked, is there?"

"No, Joe," Mark agreed. "No peace for the wicked at all." He saw the blood-shot eyes widen and Joe's Adam's apple jerk.

"You will have your little joke, Mr. Lessing, won't you? How's the Inspector? He was with you the last time you come here, wasn't he? I always said that you got a square deal from Mr. West and that goes for you, too."

"You know why I've come, we're only wasting time. You got some information about West—or you thought you did. Where did it come from?"

"What, *me?*" Joe's voice rose to a shrill falsetto. "Why, I wouldn't let a friend down, Mr. Lessing, you ought to know I wouldn't. Ha-ha-ha!" His voice cracked halfway through the laugh and he glanced towards the whisky bottle. "Why, what's happened to the Inspector?"

"Talk quickly, Joe," urged Mark.

"I can't tell you a thing, Mr. Lessing! If someone has been spreading lies about Mr. West, it wasn't me. I'm no squealer. Listen to me, Mr. Lessing, I might be able to *help* you!" He raised the bottle high, in a grand gesture. "What about that?"

"Who gave you information about West?"

"I tell you I don't know what—"

"Joe," said Mark, "you're frightened of your own shadow. Have you upset the Masher?"

He uttered the name "Masher" simply because he had heard the old man outside use it and had wondered what it implied. But he was astonished at its effect on Leech, who dropped heavily into his chair, his hands shaking. He raised the bottle to his lips and gulped; a trickle of whisky escaped them and ran down his chin, soaking into the neck of his pajamas. When he put the bottle down he almost knocked it over.

"So the Masher frightened you," murmured Mark.

"You—you don't understand," muttered Leech, "you don't understand, Mr. Lessing! There's a fella they call the Masher who thinks I welshed on him. He says he's coming after me."

Leech's color was grey. "He'll learn the truth one of these days and then it'll be all right. Mr. Lessing, if I was some people I'd ask the police for protection, that's what I would do, but I wouldn't sink so low. I've got a headache this morning. The Masher tried to beat me up last night and made me nervous."

"If the Masher is who I think he is, you'll get more than a beating up." Mark shrugged. "I might be able to help, in return for information."

"How do *you* know the Masher?" gasped Leech.

"I'm very interested in you and your friends." Mark stubbed out his cigarette and lit another. Leech did not smoke. "What name does he go by to you?"

Leech's little eyes narrowed.

"You sure you know him, Mr. Lessing?"

"I know him well enough to have him put inside, Joe, and if he were inside he couldn't do you any harm, could he?"

Leech rose unsteadily from his chair, rounded the table and approached Mark. When he was a yard away the stench of whisky was nauseating. He stretched out a podgy hand and gripped Mark's coat, peering up into Mark's eyes.

"Mr. Lessing, you wouldn't lie to me," he said hoarsely, "you wouldn't play such a trick on a man in my condition, would you? Look at me! Look at me hand!" He held one hand out, shaking violently. "If you can put Malone inside I'd do anything for you."

"Where did you get the information about West?" demanded Mark. "I'll look after Malone if you tell me that."

"I'd have to look up some records. I didn't get it direct," said Leech, backing away and narrowing his eyes craftily. "It would take me two or three days, Mr. Lessing. If you could put Malone away first."

"After you've said your piece," insisted Mark.

"Now, listen, Mr. Lessing—"

From the street, floating clearly through the open window, there came the shrill blast of a whistle, not full enough for a police call. It broke the quiet outside and cut across Leech's words. He swung round and rushed to the table, pulled open the drawer and snatched up the automatic. His fingers were shaking so much that Mark stepped hastily to one side.

"That's him!" gasped Leech. "That's the Masher!"

There was a scurry of footsteps in the street. A woman cried out in alarm, someone swore, someone else laughed unpleasantly. A clattering sound followed and the swish of water and then a thud and a volley of oaths suggesting that someone had kicked over Lizzie's bucket. A heavy bang on the bar door was followed by several others and footsteps sounded on the stairs, slow and deliberate—the approach of Clay.

"Don't let them come in!" gasped Leech.

Downstairs, a door crashed open and footsteps clattered in the bar. A single loud crack, the breaking of a bottle, was followed by a pandemonium of breaking glass and strident, jeering laughter. Clay burst in, his grey face a sea of perspiration. He closed the door and shot home the bolt but before he reached Leech someone was hammering on the door. The uproar continued downstairs; judging from the sounds bottles were being flung into the street.

"Open up, Joe," a man said. Mark was surprised by the clearness with which the voice sounded above the din. "You'll only make it worse for yourself if you don't."

"Keep them out!" gasped Joe. He pointed the gun towards the door, and his finger was unsteady on the trigger. After a pause a heavy blow splintered two of the door panels and the sharp point of a pick showed; it was wrenched away, then used again. By levering the pick, a hole was made. A hand poked through and groped about for the bolt.

Leech fired at the hand.

He missed by inches; the bullet struck the wall on the side of the door but the hand was not withdrawn. The steadiness with which its owner sought for the bolt was an object lesson. Mark stepped swiftly to Leech and pushed his arm aside.

"Do you want to be charged with murder?"

"Leave me alone!" Still holding the gun, Leech jumped away

from him and fired again. By chance, he scored a hit and blood welled up on the man's finger, but the bolt was pulled back and the door flung open. A man strode in, small, neat and flashily dressed. His dark, wavy hair was glistening with brilliantine, his narrow-featured face, handsome after a fashion, was twisted contemptuously. For a long time he stood looking at Leech, who held the gun in trembling fingers but did not fire again.

"So you thought you'd keep me out," the newcomer said. His voice was cold and harsh. He strode across the room, a swagger in every step, padded shoulders of his suit swaying. Clay reared up against the wall and stared at him, terrified. Leech drew in a shuddering breath and levelled the gun but the newcomer brushed it away, contemptuously. He held up his hand, from which the blood was streaming. "That's something else I owe you, Leech." He struck the bookmaker across the face and the blood from his wounded finger splashed into Leech's eyes and dropped on his pajama jacket.

The pandemonium downstairs was increasing. A crowd had gathered outside, and Mark thought there were several brawls in progress; the police would surely arrive before long. Mark stepped towards the newcomer.

"Do you really have to do this?"

Malone turned and looked at him insolently.

"Who are you?" he demanded.

"Not a friend of Joe," said Lessing.

"It's a lie, it's a lie!" screeched Joe. "He said he could put you inside, Masher! He said he knew you and could put you inside! That's what he said!" He pointed a quivering finger at Mark, who was acutely aware of the menace in Malone's eyes. He knew that, true to his nature, Leech had seen a chance of buying safety with information. The snide went on shouting until Malone shot out a hand and struck him across the lips. Although he still held the gun, Leech made no attempt to use it. He backed against the wall.

"Is that true?" Malone demanded.

"Do you often believe him?" countered Mark.

"Don't try to be funny." Malone suddenly shot out his hand. Apparently he expected Mark to be as hypnotized as Leech; certainly he did not expect Mark's quick evasive action, nor the clenched fist which knocked his hand aside. He did not change his expression, nor did he strike out again.

"I came to see Leech on private business," Mark said. "He was frightened out of his wits by you. I told him I could put you inside to make him give me some information. Take that or leave it." He spoke with commendable nonchalance.

Leech moaned: "It's a lie, Masher. He come to ask me about you, wanted to know more about you, said he could—"

From the landing there came a sharp report. Mark heard it and turned his head. He thought he saw a movement by the door but could not be sure; he did hear a man running down the stairs until the sound of his progress was drowned by the new outburst of noise below. He looked round—and there was Leech sliding down the wall, eyes wide open and terrified, hands clutching at his chest.

The Masher asked: "Who did that?" but stood sneering at the bookmaker as he slid to the floor and began to gasp for breath.

8

The Taxi-Driver's Memory

Mark was fascinated by the sneer on Malone's face. He felt quite sure that the man had arranged the shooting so that he could not become personally involved. Mark turned away from him and knelt beside Leech, pillowing the man's head in his arm.

"It's all right, Joe. Clay, fetch a doctor, and send someone here with some water and a towel." He opened the front of Leech's jacket, tightening his lips when he saw the oozing blood just above the heart. He doubted whether a doctor could save the man's life. Malone stood there until Lizzie came in. She flounced past him, carrying an enamel pail of water and a towel. Mark glanced up in time to see Malone pinch her waist. She jerked her head away, deposited the pail and towel and went out, making a wide detour to avoid the flash crook. At the door, she turned and put her tongue out, then disappeared.

Joe Leech was muttering but Mark could not distinguish the words. He knew that he would not learn the name of the man who had paid Leech to frame Roger. He stopped the bleeding by folding the towel and holding it over the wound but he felt helpless and out of his depth. He caught Malone's eye and the overdressed man grinned at him. It was quieter downstairs but a shrill voice called: "Police!" The Masher made no attempt to get away but pushed his hands into his pockets and watched Leech's face, distorted in pain, with an inhuman curiosity. The plump body grew convulsed, Leech began to struggle and tried to shout—only to relax, gasping for breath before becoming very still. His eyes closed—opened again—and became slack.

"He's dead," stated Malone. "There isn't much I don't know about Leech, and I'll sell what you want to know—at a price. Just ask for Masher Malone." He walked across the room and went out, without glancing behind him, as a stentorian voice bellowed up the stairs:

"Leech! You up there, Leech?"

Clay, who was nearer the door, called stiffly.

"He's been shot."

"Cripes!" exclaimed the man with the stentorian voice and he hurried up the stairs. Mark was not surprised to see his uniform as he entered. "So Joe's got it," the man said and looked curiously at Mark, as out of place there as a peacock in a poultry run. "Malone, don't you go," he called.

"I should worry," came Malone's voice.

"How'd it happen?" the policeman asked, taking it so calmly that Mark knew he was not even mildly surprised. "Was it Malone?"

"Malone was in here when the shot came from the door," Mark said. "He didn't fire it."

"And doesn't know who did fire it, copper," Malone said from the door. "I came to ask Leech some questions but before the louse could answer someone who didn't like him got busy."

More policemen arrived and statements were taken. While Mark was making his, an ambulance and two police cars drew up, finger-print and cameramen invaded the "Saucy Sue."

It was an hour before Mark was given permission to leave. None of the Divisional men recognized him or his name, to his satisfaction, for he did not want this affair linked with Roger West yet. He was glad, too, that the situation was taken out of his hands.

Clay spoke slowly when questioned. Several times he looked towards the dead body of his master. Mark wondered what queer twist of loyalty had bound Clay to the bookmaker. Mark asked no questions and kept himself in the background; consequently he knew nothing of the extensive inquiries, although when he reached the bar, he saw three plainclothes sergeants talking to three members of the pub's staff, recently come on duty.

The broken glass had been swept to either side of the bar so as to make a path. The floor was swimming in beer and spirits and the stench was overpowering to Mark's fastidious nose. The shelves were wrecked but one empty bottle stood untouched near the end of the bar—it seemed to be the only whole one left. The beer-taps had been opened and kept open, otherwise so much beer could not have escaped. Mark hurried across the room, crunching glass underfoot. Rose Street, that morning, was a place of fresh air and beauty compared with the interior of the inn.

An excited crowd had gathered and half a dozen policemen kept the gangway clear. At the front of the crowd was the old man, still in shirt and trousers and worn boots, chattering to himself. Mark looked at him narrowly, decided that it was not the time to ask him questions, and stalked off. Loud hoots of derision followed him.

He did not go to the river but towards Mile End Road and, near Aldgate Station, he found a taxi. He went straight to Chelsea and when the cab drew up outside the Wests' house he saw Roger at the window. Roger came hurrying along the path as Mark paid off his cab.

Mark turned and then missed a step, he was so startled by the expression on Roger's face.

"What—" he began.

"Have you seen Janet?" Roger demanded. His eyes were hard and glittering.

"No," Mark said, and sharp alarm cut through him.

Roger drew a deep breath. "I hoped she'd decided to come and give you a hand," he said. "She should have been here about twelve. It's half-past one now and there's no sign of her."

"Have you done anything?" Mark asked as they reached the front room.

"I've told Pep and phoned Cornish," Roger said. "Janet left Cornish at half-past eleven and as far as he knew she was coming straight back here. Mark, last night you suggested that they might be trying to get at Janet as well as me. What made you think so? Was it anything more than the fact that she was supposed to have made those payments?"

"It was a passing idea, that's all. Confound it, nothing could have happened to Janet!"

"Couldn't it?" growled Roger.

"She'll turn up. She's probably had a brainwave and gone to try to solve the mystery herself! It's not two hours yet, old man, you're worrying yourself over nothing. Did Pep have anything else to say?"

Roger pursed his lips and stared, his eyes filled with shadows. The ticking of the mantelpiece clock seemed loud, the sound of people passing in the street was very noticeable. They did not speak for fully three minutes; then Roger moved, snapping his fingers.

"What did you say?"

"Did Pep tell you anything new?"

"No. I rang him up because Cornish had identified the taxi-driver for me and I've sent him to interview the fellow." His tension appeared to relax as he smiled at Mark and added: "You've had a morning on the tiles, haven't you?"

"Do I smell of beer?" asked Mark.

"You smell as if you've been swimming in it!" Roger declared, and then: "What about Leech?"

Mark in turn looked so grim that Roger broke off. He had to wait for what seemed a long time before the other, speaking quietly, told him what had happened to Joe, and the smashing up of the "Saucy Sue" and the character of Masher Malone.

When he finished, Roger said, slowly:

"Malone impressed you, didn't he?"

"He made me look over my shoulder all the way here from the pub," Mark admitted. "Do you know him?"

"I've heard of him," said Roger. "He leads a gang but he's

never been inside. Racecourse stuff and probably some fencing. I didn't know he was big."

"If he isn't, he will be," Mark said. "He might be bigheaded but he's also got guts."

"It's Corny's old Division, he'll know what there is to know about Malone," Roger said.

"Can't you pull him in for today's trouble? Malone sent his gang to wreck the pub, beyond doubt."

"I'll bet you the actual wreckers weren't caught, and no one will identify them—the locals will be too scared of the Masher. He undoubtedly arranged for the murder to take place when he was in the room, so that the police couldn't touch him for that, although they might get him for disturbing the peace. He would probably admit that the gang got out of hand and smashed up the place but"—Roger was frowning and moving to and fro on his heels—"the very fact that he was behind the wrecking would suggest that he knew nothing of intent to murder."

"Why?"

Roger said: "He, or his gang, had a grievance against Leech, probably because he's squealed and put one or two of them inside. The Masher's retort was to break Leech's place up—an eye for an eye. But if he intended murder, would he trouble to do the wrecking?"

"Would the court accept that argument?"

"Not if we could prove anything else against Malone, but I think he'll have made sure we can't. What did you actually see him do?"

"Unbolt the door and strike Leech," Mark said.

"It's hardly a crime to strike someone who's threatening to shoot you," Roger said.

"Surely the Division will hold him for questioning."

"Oh, yes, but with a good lawyer he'll get off even if he is taken as far as the court, but I doubt whether the case will be allowed to go so far. If the Division arrests and charges him and he gets off, it would be more difficult to get him on a similar charge afterwards. Even the biggest rogue can claim that he's being persecuted and get a lot of public and judiciary sympathy!" He laughed, rather acidly. "Never become a policeman, Mark!"

After a pause, Mark asked quietly:

"Is that as far as you'll go?"

"Except for questions." Roger was brisk. "Why did it coincide with your arrival? Pub wrecking is a pastime that's indulged in often enough, but usually it's done after dark, when the pub is open. In the confusion the gang can escape and the police get tangled up with the innocent customers who've joined in for the fun of the thing. A morning mob attack is rare."

"It surely can't have had anything to do with me."

"I think it almost certainly had. You probably saw no one on the way to the pub, but a hundred people saw you go in. If Malone wanted to make sure Leech didn't squeal about him he'd have lookers-out everywhere and would know within five minutes that you'd arrived. You say there was a whistle and Leech knew immediately that it was a sign of Malone?"

"Yes. But how the dickens could he have known of me?"

"Mind not working well this morning?" Roger asked. "If Malone was connected with the attempt to frame me he would know that you've often lent me a hand."

Mark stared. "I can't believe—"

The telephone rang. Roger started, and stepped swiftly forward. "There is a call for you," said the operator. "Hold on, please." Roger heard her speaking to the caller. "Press Button A, please—you're through."

"Roger!" cried Janet.

"Thank God you're all right," said Roger, sitting down heavily on the arm of a chair. Mark saw perspiration on his forehead and an inane grin on his lips. "Jan, where—"

"I've had the very dickens of a time!" Janet said. "I've never been so scared. I'm at Chertsey."

"Chertsey!"

"I left Cornish and thought I would walk across St. James's and get a bus from Victoria Street. I was in the park when two men came alongside me." Janet spoke breathlessly. Roger's smile faded and his lips set in a grim line. "They told me to obey them if I wanted to be unhurt—Roger, it was fantastic! There were hundreds of people about and there was I walking between them, not daring to raise my voice. They hired a taxi, made me get in, and climbed in after me. And Roger, they just didn't speak! It was awful. Whenever I started to say anything they told me to be quiet."

"Go on," said Roger, tautly.

"It seemed an unending journey," Janet said. "I felt sure that I was being kidnapped. Once I thought I might jump out, at a traffic jam, but one of them gripped my arm and I couldn't do a thing. We reached Hounslow, and they made me get out, took me to another taxi and—brought me here."

"And then?" Roger asked.

"*Nothing!*" exclaimed Janet.

"Nothing at all?" Roger sounded incredulous.

"Absolutely nothing. They stopped the taxi outside one of the houses by the river—the phone number of the kiosk is Chertsey 123 but it's not far from Staines—and told me to get out. Then they drove off! I walked along the river and came to this kiosk."

"Well, thank God it's no worse," Roger said. "Get to Staines and come to Waterloo. I'll meet you there. I'll find the times of trains." He turned to a writing cabinet but Mark was already at it, taking out a time-table. He turned the pages and gave the times of the trains and Roger repeated them.

"I'll catch the three something," Janet said. "I haven't had any lunch and I'm starved. Don't trouble to meet me, I'll be all right."

"Get a snack at the station buffet and catch the two something," Roger said firmly. "I won't be happy until I set eyes on you . . . Yes, I do mean it! . . . Oh, we'll have a snack here, Mark has had an alarming morning, too . . . Yes, I will . . . Good-bye for now."

He replaced the receiver and turned to Mark.

"Warning Number 1, or 2, or 3, choose which you like!"

"Warning?" ejaculated Mark.

"They've demonstrated that they can make Janet do a disappearing trick," Roger said. "It can't mean anything else. At least we know that they mean business!" He smiled more freely and led the way to the kitchen. "We'd better get a snack."

It was a quarter to two and Janet's train was not due to arrive at Waterloo until after three. Nothing happened meanwhile and Roger set out for Waterloo. He reached the station ten minutes before the train arrived and could hardly wait. When the train came in and Janet was not among the first passengers, he peered along the platform anxiously, trying to distinguish her tall figure. He was about to push through the barrier when he caught sight of her, quite outstanding amongst the motley crowd.

They gripped hands and Roger drew her towards him and kissed her.

"I've never known a journey take so long," Janet said.

"You *are* all right?" Roger demanded.

"Bruised only in spirit," Janet said, and laughed with relief. "What on earth did they do it for? To show what they *can* do if they make up their minds?"

"Probably," Roger agreed. "But we aren't going to let it worry us now, and I'm going to keep you on a piece of string until this is over!" He looked at her and saw that her eyes were filled with tears. "Oh, my sweet!"

"No, don't fuss me!" Janet said, sharply for her.

He walked quietly by her side, thinking that the experience had affected her more than he would have expected. Soon, she tucked her arm into his.

"Sorry," she said, "I feel so jumpy."

"Who wouldn't?" Roger asked.

They said little as he drove home, except that Janet did her best to describe the two men who had forced her into the taxi.

As they turned into Bell Street they saw a taxi waiting

outside the house. Roger's thoughts were diverted. He gripped Janet's arm and hustled her along.

"Who do you think has called?" demanded Janet.

"A cabby with a good memory, I hope," said Roger. "Ah, there's Pep! It's my man of last night all right!"

9

An Address in Welbeck Street

The cabby was a gruff individual, as Roger remembered from their brief encounter in the black-out. He was also stolid and solid. He wore a dirty collar and tie but only one overcoat; he was with Pep Morgan and Mark in the lounge and glared at Roger as he entered but he managed to smile when he saw Janet, and touched his forehead. He even removed his cap.

"Now p'raps you can tell me what it's all about?" he said, eyeing Roger aggressively. "I dunno wot you think I am. Got to be earning me living, I have, not like some people." He sniffed.

"Do you remember taking me to Scotland Yard last night?" Roger asked, taking out his wallet and extracting two pound notes. The cabby sniffed again, and answered more affably:

"Yes, Guv'nor. I remember."

"And you let another man share the cab?"

"I don't 'ave to tell yer what you already know, Guv'nor, do I?"

"I'm talking as a private citizen," Roger said. "How far did the other man go?"

"West End," said the cabby.

"Do you remember where you dropped him?"

"Yers—end of Welbeck Street."

"Did he say where he was going from there?"

"No," said the cabby. "He just said the end of Welbeck Street would be all right for 'im. He went down the street. I know that, 'cos I saw him disappear into a house. I wanted to lay orf for an hour so I follered 'im along to the nearest rank."

Roger's heart began to beat fast.

"Was it far along?"

"I don't exactly know, but it wasn't so far, Guv'nor. I couldn't say for certain which one it was. Tell you what," he added, his eyes on the two pounds. "There was an island in the middle of the road just abaht where he turned into the house. I know that place like the palm of me hand. It might have been the second island or the first, but it was an island."

"That's a great help," said Roger. "Take us to Welbeck Street, will you? Pep, will you come with me?"

"Why, of course," said Morgan.

"But—" began Janet.

"Mark will look after the house," said Roger. "He'll also keep an eye on you! I won't be long." He was followed by the cabby and Pep.

"*Now* what's got into you, Handsome?" demanded Morgan. "That's the trouble with you, I never know whether I'm coming or going."

"Oh, we're going," said Roger, expansively. "And I'm full of ideas. How did you get on at the Yard last night?"

"I didn't like it much," Morgan admitted frankly. "I never did like Abbott, and after the way he talked to me I'll never have a good word to say for him. Sarcastic swine. But I didn't give anything away and you put me all right your end, Mr. Lessing says."

"They also know you're working for me," Roger said. "Have you heard what happened to Mark this morning?"

"A bit of it," said Morgan. "The driver was with us most of the time, so he couldn't say much. What *did* happen?"

Roger told him but did not add why he had suddenly become animated and left the house in such a hurry until they reached the end of Welbeck Street. The cabby explained at some length where he thought the passenger had gone. It was into one of the houses near the second island in the middle of the street.

"Thanks," Roger said. "If you care to wait, I'll probably want to go back to Chelsea soon."

"I don't mind waiting," said the cabby.

"Would you mind telling me what you think you can do at a house where this man *might* have come?" demanded Morgan. "I can't help you if I'm in the dark all the time, Handsome, can I?"

"Pep, you missed a vision this morning," said Roger, in high good humor. "A Daimler pulled up outside my house and out the vision stepped."

"Now be sensible."

"Oh, I am being! She was beauty itself and there was money oozing from her. She came, she said, to solicit Janet's help for the Society of European Relief. Oddly enough," he added, offhandedly, "the offices of the Society are in Welbeck Street."

Morgan looked at him sharply.

"So I wouldn't be surprised if we don't find many interesting things here," said Roger. "We've plenty to go on, Pep. How do you like working for an ex-policeman?"

"Now don't talk like that," remonstrated Morgan. "What are you going to do now?"

"You take the next house, I'll take the one beyond it," Roger said. "See if you can find the name of the Society of European Relief on one of the boards." He smiled as Pep went up four steps leading to an open door and whistled to himself as he viewed the house next door. It had been taken over as offices but none of the name boards mentioned the Society. To refresh his memory, he looked at Mrs. Sylvester Cartier's card: Welbeck Street was right but there was no number. Pep passed him, shaking his head. They were opposite the island and the cabby had pulled up on the other side of the road.

The next house was a blank also, but when Roger walked down the steps he saw Morgan standing on the porch next door, waving. Roger joined him quickly.

"Got it!" exclaimed Morgan. "You'll make quite a detective when you grow up, Handsome!" He led the way into a darkened hallway and pointed to the notice board, which had the names of four different firms or institutions; on the third floor—the top—was the Society of European Relief. "But there's no lift," Morgan mourned.

"I couldn't ask you to walk up all those stairs," Roger said. "Stay down here and keep your eyes open."

"Now listen—"

"You can't have it all your own way," Roger told him. He made for the stairs, going up the first flight two at a time but then proceeding more calmly. Pep did not attempt to follow.

The landings were darkened but windows were open and allowed some light in. On the third floor a typewriter was clattering and one door was ajar. It was marked "Inquiries" and had the name of the Society underneath. Roger stepped in. Behind a wooden partition he could hear a typewriter going at great speed. He pressed a bell in the counter and started at the loud, harsh ring. The typewriter stopped at the first sound, a chair was pushed back and a girl rounded the partition.

She was pretty; she wore a white blouse and a dark skirt; her hair was dark, like Janet's, and she was about Janet's height. She appeared very self-possessed, and smiled pleasantly. On her right hand was a solitaire diamond ring, a beautiful thing.

"Good afternoon, sir. Can I help you?" Roger liked her voice.

"I think you probably can," he said.

"In what way, please?"

Roger smiled disarmingly. "I wonder if you would take £250 in notes to the Mid-Union Bank and put it into my account? My name is West."

He knew at once that he had scored a hit. The girl backed away, her eyes narrowed, and he thought she groped behind her as if for help. As he gave his name, her lips—red but not heavily made-up—parted slightly and her breathing grew agitated.

"What—what are you talking about?" she demanded.

"Don't tell me that I have to say it again," said Roger. "After all, you've done it often enough to know how easy it is, haven't you?"

"You're talking nonsense!"

"I wonder how long you'll continue to think so?"

"If you have any business to discuss, please state what it is," said the girl stiffly. She stood a foot away from the counter with her hands clenched by her sides; the ring glittered like fire; she was badly frightened, but she tried hard not to show it and her voice was steady. "I haven't time to waste."

"You know," said Roger, "the bank cashier will be able to identify you."

"I have no idea what you mean. Please go away."

"What, so soon?" asked Roger. "I've only just—"

A door behind the partition began to open; he could see the top of it. Someone moved towards the reception office and a middle-aged man appeared, the expression on his kindly face looking faintly puzzled. He had grey hair and a gentle voice.

"Lois, my dear," he said, "I thought you were going to—oh!" he broke off at sight of Roger. "I beg your pardon, I did not know you were engaged. Can we help you, sir?"

Roger beamed. "Can I give you a lift? I'm going as far as Scotland Yard."

"I *beg* your pardon!"

"Do you know, I think you are both being wilfully obtuse," Roger said, as if wonderingly, "but you'll have to change your attitude."

"I dislike your threatening manner, sir!"

"No threats," Roger said, "just a little jogging of your memory. Last night you begged a lift in my cab, and—"

"I was at home *all* last night," interrupted the man, giving sufficient emphasis to the "all" to make it clear that he was confident of his alibi. "Lois, has this person been threatening you?"

The girl said, hesitantly: "He seems to think he knows me."

"Do you know him?"

"No."

"You will both know me in future," Roger said. He looked them up and down, then turned and left the office. The door, which was fitted with a vacuum-type doorstop, closed behind him with a gentle hiss.

He was no longer smiling. He had bungled a golden opportunity, and allowed himself to be carried away by a bright idea, in a way which would have disgraced a raw sergeant. He should have made a tentative inquiry and then engineered an opportunity for the bank cashier to see the girl; now, he had warned them of their danger, had virtually invited them to get away.

He had made another mistake, too; he should have brought Morgan up with him, the little man should now be waiting outside the door, ready to slip inside and listen-in to the conversation in the inner office. He reached the head of the stairs, then stopped, for Morgan was smiling at him from halfway up the stairs!

"You were away so long that I thought—"

"Hush!" warned Roger, beckoning. Morgan drew level. "Try to get inside the office, the first on the right, and hear what's being said next door. They won't hear you go in if you're careful."

Morgan hurried past him.

Easier in his mind, Roger went to the first landing and stood by the banisters, lighting a cigarette. He was really angry with himself; had it been Mark, he could have forgiven it. He had been wrong to come here, Mark should have handled this part of the inquiry. He admitted ruefully that from the moment when the idea of the Welbeck Street association had first entered his head he had been carried away by it and, on finding that he had scored a hit, had let himself be dazzled by the success of the visit.

He heard someone coming up the stairs.

He thought at once of Mrs. Sylvester Cartier and looking round hastily, saw a door, marked "Inquiries," of another suite; he slipped inside. Keeping the door open an inch or two he looked out, but as the newcomer drew nearer he felt sure that he had been wrong. Mrs. Cartier would walk with a brisk step and her heels would tap sharply on the bare wooden boards. This walker came slowly.

It was a man, whose careworn face was lined with the marks of great suffering. His sad eyes and the dejected droop of his shoulders startled Roger. He watched the man walking wearily towards the next flight of stairs and then realized that the newcomer would almost certainly discover Pep.

An exclamation behind him told him that he had been seen and he stepped swiftly out of the office, closing the door. He hurried after the haggard man.

"Excuse me, sir."

"Yes?" The man's European accent was strong.

"I thought I would save you wasting a journey," Roger said. "There is no one in upstairs—I have just been trying to get in myself."

Sad, disappointed eyes regarded him, making him ashamed of the lie.

"T'ank you, sir, t'ank you so mooch." The man ran his fingers through his sparse hair. "I vill vait, I t'ink. I 'ave come for an app—appointment." He looked along the bare passage and, at the far end, Roger saw some benches. "I weel sit down, please."

"Oh, by all means!" said Roger. "I'll wait with you."

The benches were at the far end of the passage. Roger thought he heard a mutter of conversation but could not be sure. The old fellow shuffled along beside him, weary and broken. Roger offered him a cigarette but he declined.

Nor did Roger receive any encouragement when he tried to start a conversation. After a quarter of an hour he began to wonder whether anything had happened to Pep. He grew alarmed and excused himself and moved towards the doors. One opened, and Pep came out on tip-toe. He hurried along the passage but faltered when he saw Roger, who shook his head. Pep took his meaning and hurried down the stairs.

"Well, that's surprising!" exclaimed Roger. "No one answered when I knocked."

"It ees—your turn," the old man said, in a tone of infinite patience.

"I'm in no hurry," said Roger. "You go first."

"You—you weel not mind?" The man was startled, but when Roger reassured him he walked more briskly towards the end of the passage and disappeared into the office. Once he had gone, Roger hurried in Morgan's wake. The private detective was standing on the pavement, near the taxi, and the cabby was speaking bitterly to him of the lack of consideration displayed by some people. He stood to attention when Roger arrived and asked sarcastically:

"Any more waiting, *sir?*"

"No," said Roger, briefly. "Back to Bell Street." He looked at Morgan.

"Bell Street's all right for me," said Morgan. When they were sitting together in the cab he shot a sideways glance at Roger, full of meaning. "Handsome, have we found something big," he breathed.

Roger said tensely: "What?"

"That was the girl who paid in the cash, and you've scared the wits out of her," said Morgan. "The old man did most of the talking, but I couldn't hear all of it. He tried to pacify her at first but didn't have much luck. But—" Morgan's little eyes were rounded with concern—"he put the fear of death into her then."

"Well, well!" said Roger, softly.

"When she kept saying that she couldn't do any more he told her she knew what he could do to her if she didn't behave herself and ordered her to go back to her work. I came out then, I didn't think she'd be long after me."

"Pep, we ought to have waited, I can't do anything right today. We'll have to follow her."

Morgan grinned. "I've got her address! Her handbag was on her desk, so I had a peek inside it. I think I've got his private address, too—she called him Pickerell; you couldn't mistake a name like that, could you? I found a "Pickerell" in an address book on her desk and made a note of it. Her name is Randall."

Sitting back at ease and copying the addresses in his notebook, Roger said:

"You're teaching me my job, Pep!"

"Who's surprised?" asked Morgan, heavily. "Handsome, what have we struck? I didn't catch a glimpse of the girl but I don't mind telling you I felt sorry for her."

"I know what you mean."

"Well, as we know who paid the money in, that lets you out," said Morgan. "But *they* know you know and that makes it awkward. Then, why did that vision you talked about virtually tell you to go there? I know she didn't actually tell you, but she went pretty near it, didn't she?"

"She did," admitted Roger, frowning. "And—Pep, we're crazy!" He leaned forward and rapped on the glass partition, opening it as the cabby automatically applied his brakes. "Back to Welbeck Street quick!" Roger ordered, startling the man so much that he was unable to find a comment.

"She's our evidence," Roger said to Morgan. "She's close to breaking-point; Pickerell knows it. I wouldn't like to be responsible for what will happen to her if we leave her with him for long."

"Oh my God!" gasped Morgan.

"He knows that if I bring Yard men along and question her persistently enough the place will be closed down, the whole racket might be broken open," Roger said. "He'll see that she's the weak link, and—" he broke off, not needing to explain further, and sat on the edge of the seat, tightlipped.

They reached Welbeck Street sooner than he expected, and pulled up with a jerk outside the house where the Society had offices. The driver looked round with an expression which said: "Does *that* satisfy you?" but Roger was already getting out. He ran up the steps and disappeared up the stairs. As he neared the top landing he heard voices, including that of the girl. Breathing hard, he turned the corner and saw the old fellow who had gone in ahead of him. There was a brighter expression on the careworn face, and he smiled at Roger, not widely but with some relief.

The door was closing.

Roger opened it and made so much noise that the girl, who could hardly have sat down after seeing the old man off, came round the partition.

Her face dropped. He could see the signs of strain in her eyes and knew that Morgan had been right, that she was afraid. Yet something in Roger's expression seemed to affect her and she did not cry out.

Roger spoke quietly:

"Don't take risks, Miss Randall. Get out while the going's good."

She gulped. "I—I don't understand you."

Roger said: "You do, you're as frightened as you can be. I heard the conversation and—"

"*Did* you?" asked the man named Pickerell. He was at the partition, his face still looked gentle and his eyes were half hidden by his glasses, but nothing hid the automatic in his right hand. "You are very impetuous, Mr. West, aren't you? I think it's time that we reached an understanding. Go into my office, Lois. Mr. West, don't do anything foolish, I am quite capable of shooting you. Just follow Miss Randall."

10

The Mistake of Mr. Pickerell

Disobeying a desperate man with a gun was not Roger's idea of common sense. He obeyed without looking behind him, hoping that Pep had followed close enough to have overheard.

"Stand over by the window," ordered Pickerell.

"I hope you realize that you're asking for trouble," Roger said.

"Perhaps not the first time, and I know how far I can go." The thought seemed to amuse him. "And you are no longer a policeman with authority, Mr. West; I have heard of your discomfiture."

"Oh," said Roger, softly: "You learned very quickly, didn't you?"

"It doesn't do to lose time," said Pickerell. "We won't waste any now, either. Let me sum up the situation. You think that by exerting enough pressure you can persuade Miss Randall to clear you of the suspicion of paying money into your account at the Mid-Union Bank. You think that by so doing you can regain your position at Scotland Yard and use the forces of law to attack *me*. Think again, Mr. West!"

Roger did not speak. The girl stood by the desk, her troubled eyes narrow and looking at Roger intently. She drummed the fingers of her left hand on the corner, making the diamonds in the engagement ring scintillate.

"Think again," repeated Pickerell. "Miss Randall was the

actual messenger, but someone gave her the money. She might be persuaded to say that it was you. In fact I think I can rely on her to do that. Can't I, Lois?"

The girl said nothing.

"Can't I?" insisted Pickerell, sternly. "After all, my dear, you have so much at stake. Nothing will happen to you, although West obviously thinks that you are in danger. You would be, if you could go free and say what you liked, but I know you will obey instructions now as you have in the past. *Won't* you?" His voice grew silky.

"I—" began the girl, and then turned away, exclaiming: "Oh, God. Yes, I will."

Pickerell smiled: "You see, Mr. West? If you tell your friends what you have discovered, or pretend to do any such thing, when Lois is questioned she will tell them exactly what they want to know. I hardly know how you have succeeded in staying free for so long, but if you want to retain that freedom, be discreet about this visit. Do you understand?"

Roger leaned back against the wall, not speaking.

"I see that you do," said Pickerell. "There is another question and I insist on an answer. If you refuse one I shall arrange for Miss Randall to tell her story whatever you do. How did you come to find this address?"

"You were traced here."

"Yes, yes, but how?"

"Your habit of slipping messages into coat pockets betrayed you. The taxi-driver was traced, and all the offices here and in the adjoining buildings were searched. Your voice is unmistakable."

"Now don't lie to me," said Pickerell. "You didn't hear my voice until after you had identified Lois."

"I talked to all girls on the premises who might have been mistaken for my wife," Roger said, plausibly. "Pickerell, there is a powerful organization at the Yard and you won't get away with this. Your gun won't help you."

"Perhaps not," said Pickerell. "But you're not a fool, West.

You won't take the risk of Lois committing perjury. Are you sure that is the way you discovered this office?"

"Yes," lied Roger.

The man seemed relieved.

"Now be sensible and go away. I suggest a long holiday in the country. I think I can assure you that when I have finished my job you will have nothing to worry about. The truth can be told afterwards, and you will be back at your desk without a stain on your character!"

Roger said: "You've made one mistake."

"Bluff will not—"

"It's nothing to do with bluff," said Roger. "You've assumed that only I heard your conversation with Miss Randall. Someone else did, too. My word might not be sufficient but the testimony of two people will. When Miss Randall realizes that her evidence will be rebutted she'll see that the only way out is to tell the truth."

The man seemed to stiffen.

"Don't lie to me."

Roger raised his voice.

"Pep, are you there? Be careful, this man's armed."

"I've rung the Yard, Handsome," came Pep's voice. "They won't be long."

The girl gasped. Pickerell backed to his desk and, keeping the gun trained on Roger, the girl and the door, who were all in line with one another he pulled open a drawer and took out some papers. He felt inside the drawer as if to make sure that it was empty, then stuffed the papers into his pocket.

Then he took out a box of matches.

Roger guessed what he intended to do, but the threat of the gun kept him still. Clumsily with one hand, Pickerell broke two matches before one ignited. He held it to the corner of a paper on the desk. It flared up. He set light to other papers. Smoke and flames rose up and began to spread.

"Don't do it!" Roger cried.

"Stay where you are!" ordered Pickerell. He moved towards a

door leading to the passage as the flames took a fiercer hold. A ring of them ran along the cable of the telephone and a draught from the open window sent two pieces of burning paper sliding along the desk where they caught others; the desk and its contents were soon ablaze, and the smoke was beginning to make Roger cough. The girl turned towards the window but Pickerell ignored her. Step by step, he reached the passage door, took a key from his pocket, inserted and turned it.

"Pep!" Roger exclaimed, moving forward, "he's—"

Pickerell stretched out a leg and kicked a chair, standing near the wall. He pulled the door open and stepped swiftly into the passage. Morgan's voice was raised and Pickerell fired. The gun had no silencer and the shot echoed loudly, followed by a sharp exclamation from Morgan. Roger leapt over the chair and reached the passage in time to see Pep leaning against the wall, holding one foot off the ground, and Pickerell disappearing down the stairs. He ran past Pep and might have caught the man up when the "Inquiries" door opened and Lois Randall appeared. She got in his way, blocking his path by accident or design. He pushed past her and sped on, calling:

"Put that fire out!"

He could not see Pickerell when he reached the street. The stocky cabby was lounging against his taxi, staring towards the Piccadilly end of the street.

"Some people!" he was saying. "Swore at me just because I said—"

"Did he get a cab?"

"Yers. 'Arf way up the road."

"You didn't hear where he was going?"

"Now what do you think I am?" demanded the cabby, with a vast, triumphant grin. "A human walkie-talkie?"

"One day you'll learn when to be funny," Roger said savagely. "Telephone Scotland Yard from the nearest callbox, ask for Inspector Cornish and tell him that West—have you got that, West?"

"Yes."

"West says that he should send men to this address quickly," Roger said. He turned and hurried upstairs, wondering whether he was too late to stop the fire from spreading. He had been forced to attempt too many things at once. There was no sign of the girl, but Pep Morgan was disappearing into the end office, from which smoke was billowing in great choking gusts. Roger hurried after him, to find him wincing as he dragged himself towards the desk, the top of which was all ablaze. He picked up a heavy ledger with one hand, and began to beat at the desk.

"All right, Pep," said Roger, "I'll get a fire extinguisher."

He was surprised to see no one else on that floor; he called out for help. Someone had smelled the fire and was on the landing below; he hurried up. He was a middle-aged man, followed by two girls and an old lady; all of them sized up the situation quickly and began to help. A cloakroom was handy for water, and within five minutes the evil smelling foam from the extinguisher covered the desk while the two girls were going round the office, beating out little fires started by the burning paper.

Pep was sitting on a chair against the wall with his right leg stuck out in front of him. Roger turned to help him but Pep shook his head and pointed to the other door. Roger went into the room where Lois had been working. He ran through the papers on her desk, picking up an address book and a telephone index. He pushed them under his coat, and made sure there was nothing else of interest. He opened a small account book and saw that the pages were headed with copperplate handwriting, admirably executed *in black drawing ink*. The entries were not all the same, some being in a neat hand which he imagined to be the girl's, but others, in drawing ink, had exactly the same characteristics as the letter from "K."

"So I don't need to look much further for him," he muttered.

He looked through the address book, found the name "Pickerell" and an address in Lambeth. He picked up the telephone, dialled the Yard and asked for Chatworth. He was told that the AC was not in. He knew that Eddie Day would shrink from taking any action without Chatworth's express wishes; Cornish was the only man to try, but Cornish had left. Accepting the inevitable, Roger asked for Abbott.

The Superintendent's voice sounded far away.

"What is it, West?"

"I have the address of a man named Pickerell," Roger said. Whatever else Abbott did he would take the message correctly. "He has admitted arranging for the payment of the money into my account, and using an employee to impersonate my wife. Pickerell has just escaped from his office. He might have gone to his home, at 81 Bligh Street, Lambeth. Is that clear?"

"Yes. But—"

"Thanks." Roger rang off, giving Abbott no chance to ask questions, and hoping he had forced an issue.

He heard men approaching and saw Cornish passing the open door. He called out, and Cornish hurried towards him.

"Much excitement," said Roger, "but I'm afraid the bird's flown."

"Flown?" Cornish's voice rose in disappointment.

"I've just phoned Abbott and told him where he might be, so you'd better stay here," Roger said, "Abbott will probably resent it if you usurp his authority."

"I don't give a damn for Abbott!" said Cornish roundly.

Roger persuaded him to stay at the office of the Society. The fire and Roger's and Morgan's evidence were enough to justify Cornish making a search. Roger kept the address book and telephone list tucked under his coat. Eventually, Roger found that the two girls of the fire-fighting party had given Pep Morgan first aid. A bullet had entered the fleshy part of his thigh. When an ambulance arrived, the doctor said confidently that it would do perfectly until the patient reached hospital.

Roger saw the little private detective off.

"Got everything you want, Handsome?" Morgan asked as he was being lifted on to a stretcher.

"Everything," Roger assured him. "I'll look in before the day's out, Pep."

"Don't you worry about me, you look after yourself," urged Morgan. "Oh, there is *one* thing, Handsome—if you wouldn't mind telling my wife. Don't want some idiot putting the wind up her."

"I'll go straight from here," Roger promised.

Pep said "Ta!," and the doors were closed on him.

Roger felt a strange independence in his freedom from the obligation to go immediately to the Yard and report, and he was appreciative of Cornish's "forgetfulness" in not telling him to stay long enough to make a full statement.

He found the cabby waiting nearby.

"Anywhere else, Guv'nor?" he asked, and then eagerly: "Your pal copped it, didn't he?"

"Oh, that was nothing to what might happen next. Shall I hire another cab?"

"Don't you leave me out o' this," snapped the cabby with quick resentment. "I drove all through the blitz, didn't I? What's a little thing like this to the blitz? Where to?"

Roger said promptly: "Clapham Common."

Then he broke off. Looking along the street, he saw a Daimler limousine turn the corner and approach. He did not know whether Mrs. Sylvester Cartier was inside but recognized her chauffeur, the man with the name of "Bott."

11

The Strange Behavior of a Beautiful Woman

As Roger stepped away from him, the cabby drew himself up to his full height, puffed out his chest and thrust forward his square, unshaven chin, narrowed his shrewd eyes and spoke with deep feeling.

"Guv'nor, *will* you make up your mind? Are you a fare or aren't you? Do you want to go to Clapham Common or don't you?"

Roger took out a handful of silver, thrust it into the cabby's hand, and said:

"Give me some change. Make it look as if I'm paying you off." He waited only for the man's startled expression to change to one of understanding before going on: "Drive along the street and wait where you can follow the Daimler when it moves off. When you've finished that, telephone a report to my Chelsea house—Chelsea 0123. Keep the chase up all night if necessary."

"Okay!" The cabby delved and found a sixpence. "There's your change, Guv'nor!"

"I'm relying on you," Roger said. "What's your name?"

"Dixon."

"All right, Dixon. I'll make the job worth your while."

The Daimler had drawn up and chauffeur Bott was standing, stiff as a ramrod, by the door. A man stepped out, tall, elegant, impressive-looking. He turned to assist Mrs. Sylvester Cartier from the car, and the two of them, a fine pair, stood together eyeing the crowd which had gathered, the policemen and the evidence of a fire.

"*Now* what has happened?" demanded the man. His voice was low-pitched but audible to Roger. "Has one of your sorrowing gentlemen lost his head?"

"Probably," said Mrs. Cartier, distantly.

She looked at Roger. There was no sign of recognition on her face but she beckoned him; it was an imperious gesture. He moved towards her, as if reluctantly. Her eyes held an expression to which he could not put a name, yet he read warning in it; the fact that she did and said nothing to suggest that she knew him might have accounted for that. She had been instrumental in bringing him here; obviously that had been the real purpose of her visit to Bell Street, and he was prepared to play her game for the time being.

"Can I help you?" he asked.

"Can you tell me what is happening here?" she asked.

"There's been a fire."

"Where?"

"On the top floor," Roger said. "No great harm was done, they soon got it under control. I think there was some other trouble," he went on. "A man was shot."

"Shot!" ejaculated the elegant man. "Great heavens! Seriously?"

"He isn't dead yet," Roger said drily.

"You see, Antoinette!" The man turned to Mrs. Cartier, his large, expressive eyes filled with concern. "This is what happens when you indulge in such whims. A shooting affray!" He turned on Roger. "Are the police up there?"

"Yes," said Roger.

"My dear," said the elegant man, sadly, "I have always told you that if you allowed your social conscience to rule your head you would one day regret it."

The woman smiled at him. "You are always so helpful, darling!" Her words and her smile held barbs. "We must go upstairs and find out what has happened. Thank you!" She smiled at Roger and then swept towards the door.

"Strewth!" exclaimed the cabby, appearing from nowhere. "Did you see 'er?"

Roger turned abruptly. Bott stood rigidly by the closed door of the Daimler, looking past Roger.

The behavior of Mrs. Cartier did nothing to help. If the cabby did a good job, however, Roger would soon know where Mrs. Cartier lived and what calls she made that day. He would not have been surprised had she decided to hurry away from the scene when she had learned what had happened but, apparently, as President of the Society she was determined to see it through. If he believed all the inferences possible from the brief conversation between her and the man—was he her husband? he wondered—the Society was a hobby which she took seriously and of which he disapproved.

He wished that he could place the man.

He strolled towards the end of the street and smoked two cigarettes before the woman reappeared, followed by her escort.

Mrs. Cartier stood outside the house and looked in either direction. Roger crossed the end of the street, seeing her out of the corner of his eye. She turned on her heel and began to walk towards him. Her escort took a few steps in her direction but she looked over her shoulder and said something which made him stop, at the side of a ladder reared against the wall. The woman had passed under it, the man stepped to one side. Then she swept along the street.

Roger walked back across the road, and they reached the corner together. She stared straight ahead but as she passed she whispered:

"I must see you tonight, at 11 Bonnock House."

She went past. A man nearby must have heard her speak, but Roger doubted whether he had heard everything. He continued walking. Mrs. Cartier raised a hand to a taxi, climbed in and was driven off. Roger did not hear what address she gave. The cabby would follow the Daimler, though, and would surely report. The elegant man had entered the Daimler which was already moving in the opposite direction. Roger saw the taxi come out of a side-street and follow it.

He hoped that Abbott would have Pickerell's home visited but decided that there was no point in going there himself. As things dropped into perspective he realized that his first job was to find Lois Randall. He toyed with the idea of telephoning Mark, but decided that it might lose precious time. He looked at his note of the girl's address—29, Chapel Street, St. John's Wood—and found a taxi.

Twenty minutes later he entered the Chapel Street house.

A board in the gloomy hall told him that the place, a large one standing in its own grounds and with an untidy garden and drive, was divided into furnished flatlets—two, said a notice, were vacant. Cards pinned against other numbers told him the names of the occupants and he found *"Miss Lois Randall"* opposite Number 9. Another sign told him that was on the third floor.

He walked up the stone steps, his heels ringing and making the quiet of the rest of the house seem ominous. He heard no other sound until he reached the door of Number 9. There were two flats on that floor, opposite each other. He heard movements inside, flurrying footsteps, voices. One was a man's, youthful and persistent—it sounded more frequently than the girl's, but hers was unmistakable.

Roger rang the bell.

The man stopped talking as the bell rang. There was a brief, startled silence before the girl said:

"Don't open it! Don't open it!"

"Lois, you can't—"

"I tell you not to open it!" she said urgently. "It might be—" she broke off.

In a low-pitched voice, the man said:

"Lois, if you won't tell me what's frightening you, how can I help?"

"You can't," she said. "Oh, Bill, please."

Roger raised his voice.

"Don't let her go out the back way. It might be dangerous for her." The words sounded melodramatic but that didn't matter. There was another short silence and then "Bill's" decisive voice.

"I'm going to see who it is."

"Bill! If you do I'll never—"

She did not finish, for "Bill's" footsteps sounded in the room and the door opened. A young man stood squarely in front of Roger. He was well-built with untidy hair and clear blue eyes. He wore a tweed coat which had seen better days, baggy flannels and an open-necked shirt; he looked as if he had just stepped out of a bath.

"Well?" he demanded. "What's all this about?"

"It's not him!" the girl cried.

"Do you mind if I come in?" Roger pushed past "Bill," who seemed so startled by the girl's reaction and the obvious relief in her voice that he made no protest. Roger closed the door and stood regarding the girl.

"Who are you?" demanded "Bill" gruffly.

"He's a policeman!" Lois exclaimed. "He came to the office to make inquiries. Bill, send him away! I won't say anything."

"Bill" growled: "You heard her."

Roger said briskly: "Supposing we behave like sensible human beings. Miss Randall will soon be hysterical if you let her go on like this and you won't help matters by threatening to punch my nose." He took out his cigarette case and offered it to the startled "Bill." The diamond ring on the girl's finger caught his eye. "I am a policeman but I am not on duty and my inquiries this afternoon were private ones. Miss Randall can help me; I hope she will."

"Send him away!" gasped Lois.

"Lois, surely you're not afraid of the police?"

"Will you tell him to go?" she flared. "Or do you want to send me to jail?"

"Nothing you have done under pressure will send you to

prison," Roger said. "I've made it clear that I'm here in a private capacity, nothing you say now will be used in evidence against you."

He heard a sharp movement in the room behind them, as if something had been knocked over. The girl turned and stared at the other door, terrified. Roger stepped to the door while "Bill" darted to the girl's side.

Roger stretched out a hand, but before he touched the handle the door opened.

He did not know why he was quite so shocked, although at the first glimpse he identified the man standing in the doorway. The man had a twisted smile on his narrow face. His hands were deep in his pockets, and he was clad in a narrow-waisted suit with padded shoulders, a gaudy tie and wide trousers. He wore no hat and his hair was carefully marcelled.

Roger thought: "Malone, for a fortune!"

"What's all the noise about?" demanded Masher Malone, swaggering forward and eyeing first Roger, then "Bill" and finally the girl. "Hallo, honey, aren't you pleased to see me? I've just come to take you for a little ride." He looked at the men again and his lips curled. "Beat it," he said. "You're in the way."

He stared at them insolently and with astounding confidence.

12

"Why So Frightened?"

Malone expected them to go. It did not seem to occur to him that they would refuse. In his wide experience, Roger had met nothing quite like this swaggering confidence.

"Bill" stared open-mouthed at him, but the expression in his eyes suggested that his temper was rapidly coming to boiling point. The girl looked only at Malone; obviously she knew him, and was terrified.

"Bill" made the first move, stepping forward and speaking in a high-pitched, wondering voice:

"Who the devil do you think you are?"

"Bill, don't argue with him!" exclaimed Lois. "Go away, please, both of you go away! I shall be all right. He's—he's a friend of mine. Yes, a friend," she repeated in a pitiful effort to sound convincing. "Don't worry about me, Bill."

"You heard her." Malone cut across her words; he put his head on one side and peered at "Bill." "I'm a friend of hers. On your way, boys."

Roger watched the younger man and saw the slow metamorphosis. At first he had felt impatient with "Bill," who seemed absurdly naïve and young for his age, but the man's eyes narrowed and his expression grew more shrewd. He closed his mouth and a wary expression filled his blue eyes. Then—the most surprising thing—he smiled faintly.

"So you're a friend of hers."

"You heard me the first time, I don't want to get rough, so be on your way."

"Bill's" smile widened.

"Come on, get rough," he invited. "Lois isn't leaving here with you, now or at any other time."

"Bill!" cried the girl.

Malone's eyes narrowed. He moved forward, sliding his feet over the carpet and taking his hands from his pockets slowly. "Bill" stood without moving, body relaxed, hands loose by his sides. Roger felt as if he were outside the situation; the girl had obviously decided that she was helpless now.

Malone stopped in front of "Bill," stared at him for an appreciable time, then moved his right hand swiftly and snapped his fingers under Bill's nose. Bill *blinked.* He did not move, he did not back away hastily nor raise his hands. Then Malone moved his knee up sharply towards Bill's groin.

Roger went forward, expecting "Bill" to be taken by surprise and stagger away. He did nothing of the kind. He swerved to one side so that Malone's knee caught him on the thick part of the thigh. At the same time he raised his hands and struck Malone on either cheek, flat-handed blows with the reports like pistol shots. Malone backed away, dumbfounded. Dark red marks showed on his cheeks and into his eyes there sprang an ugly glitter, the evil look which Roger had seen before.

Malone whipped his right hand to his waistcoat and drew out a knife.

The swift movement would have deceived most men, but "Bill" moved his right hand and chopped Malone's wrist. The knife dropped to the floor. "Bill" seemed to move his arm negligently and Malone gasped and went flying against the wall. He came up against it with a thud which shook the room and made his oily marcel waves fall over his eyes and face. "Bill" stepped forward and trod on the knife; the blade broke into several pieces.

"Would you like some more?" he inquired.

Roger chuckled, but no one took the slightest notice of him.

Malone straightened himself up, brushed his hair out of his eyes and shrugged his coat straight. More wary and with the glitter in his eyes enough to frighten most people, he approached, crouching, his hands outstretched and fingers crooked, like a wrestler. "Bill" kept quite still, relaxed and yet giving an impression of latent strength.

"Come on," taunted "Bill," "I'm waiting."

Malone flew at him, relying on speed of the movement to carry him backwards. Bill swayed to one side, gripped the man's arm again and repeated the first maneuver. This time he did not stand back after Malone hit the wall, but grabbed his left wrist and brought it behind him in a hammer-lock. He dragged Malone upright, and for the first time acknowledged Roger's presence.

"Open the door, will you?"

Roger hurried to obey.

"Thanks," said Bill, politely. He ran Malone forward, and the man could not stop himself. Roger watched them go out, saw Malone stagger down the first steps. "Bill" was clearly determined to make a thorough job of it, for he pushed the Masher down the stairs, their footsteps echoed clearly and the heavy breathing of Malone could be heard.

The girl stood rigid in the center of the room. Roger stepped swiftly to the window and drew aside the curtains. Malone was walking unsteadily in the road, obviously crossing to the opposite pavement to get further away from the human cyclone which he had released. His shoulders slumped and he was so dejected that Roger could not repress another chuckle.

"It's not funny!" cried Lois. Her eyes were blazing with anger but she was close to tears.

"Miss Randall, your friend can look after himself very well."

"You don't know what Malone will do to him!" she cried. "He'll never forgive him, it couldn't have been worse. You—you're a policeman, aren't you? You've got to help Bill, you've got to make sure that he doesn't get hurt! Malone won't forget. He'll—" she broke off.

"Go on," Roger said. "What will he do?"

"Oh, what's the use of talking! I've warned you—why didn't you stay away, why did you have to come here? I might have persuaded Bill to be sensible!"

"I doubt it," said Roger. "Who is he?"

She stared. "Who? Malone?"

"I know Malone. I mean 'Bill.' "

"He—he's just a friend of mine."

They heard "Bill" coming up the stairs, running the last few steps and coming breezily into the room, smiling with deep satisfaction. He had eyes only for Lois, although he spoke to Roger.

"My name is Tennant, and I'm more than a friend of Lois's, I am her fiancé—although sometimes she doesn't seem very sure about it!" He grinned, looking twice as confident as he had before Malone's arrival. "Sweetheart, this has got to stop, you know. I can see you've been in trouble while I've been away but it can't be as bad as you seem to think. Don't let an over-dressed lout like Malone frighten you. Should she?" he appealed to Roger.

"She certainly shouldn't. Do I gather that you've been away and come back to find Miss Randall in this spot?"

"Yes. I've been up north for several months and had no idea that this was happening until—" he paused, as if doubtful whether it was wise to go any further. "But that's none of your business. Do you mind leaving, so that Lois and I can go into things privately?"

"Yes, I do."

"I don't see why."

"You will, in time," Roger assured him. "Miss Randall has been persuaded to contribute one or two things towards ruining my reputation at Scotland Yard. I've a deep personal interest."

"I don't believe it!" Tennant said. He looked at Lois with a puzzled expression in his eyes. He was more like he had been when Roger had first arrived.

Tears filmed her eyes. She turned away, her shoulders

shaking, and blindly walked into another room. She did not close the door after her and Roger saw her fling herself, face downwards, on a single bed.

"Oh, lord!" exclaimed Tennant, stepping towards her.

Roger laid a hand on his arm.

"I shouldn't," he advised. "Leave her for a few minutes. Is there a telephone in the flat?"

"There's one on the next floor—a public call-box."

"I'll be back in a few minutes," Roger said. "Tennant, don't let Lois leave here. Don't encourage her, don't let her persuade you to take her out the back way. If you're gone when I come back there'll be more trouble than you expect, and she won't be safe unless she's with friends all the time."

Tennant looked steadily into his eyes, then nodded and said:

"I'll keep her here, don't worry."

"Good man!" Roger hurried downstairs. He found the phone on the landing and took out some coppers. There was no sound of movement in the house. He kept his eyes on the stairs leading to the street, not convinced that Malone would accept even temporary defeat. He dialed his own number, grew worried because there was no immediate answer, and was already imagining disaster at Chelsea when he heard Janet's voice.

"This is Chelsea 0123."

"Good afternoon, Mrs. West," said Roger. "I am in great need of feminine assistance to take charge of a damsel in distress. I cast my mind round and after much deliberation decided that I knew no one better qualified for the post than you, so—"

"Oh, you fool!"

Roger heard Mark's voice, Janet telling Mark to be quiet, then he went on:

"I'm at 29, Chapel Street, St. John's Wood, and I think Mark had better come with you. Will you hurry, darling?"

"I'll come like the wind! I—oh, I had the wind up thoroughly, Cornish telephoned and said that Pep had been shot and he wanted to speak to you. *Has* he been shot?"

Roger sorted out the confusion.

"Yes, but I haven't! Jan, just a moment. A quarter of an hour won't make any difference, so before you come here go to Pep's home, will you? Tell his wife that he's been shot in the leg but I'm not sure what hospital he's at."

"It's the London," Janet said in a strained voice. "Cornish told me."

"Oh, good! Will you let her know and tell her not to worry?"

"Yes." Janet rang off and Roger replaced the receiver, scratched his ear, then walked slowly up to the top flat.

Tennant was still in the outer room, looking bewildered and peering through at Lois, who was sobbing less violently but who had not moved. Roger looked about the poorly-furnished bedroom. There was a small window, fairly high up—he did not think there was any chance of her getting out that way, nor of anyone breaking in. He closed the door and turned to Tennant.

"You do take things into your own hands, don't you?" Tennant remarked.

"In this case I must," Roger said, offering a cigarette. "How much do you know?"

"Nothing. I've been in Scotland for four months. I'm—" he grinned—"an unarmed combat instructor! Before I left, Lois was—well, she was just her normal self. As a matter of fact," he added with some embarrassment, "we'd got engaged during my last leave and I was rather in the clouds, you know. Her letters didn't say anything about what's been happening but a friend of mine wrote and told me that she seemed to be badly worried. He didn't know what it was about. I didn't say anything about coming down, but I managed to wangle a week's leave earlier than I'd expected. I found—well, she's as jumpy as a cat! I thought she would fall through the floor when she saw me. Then I realized that some brutes are pestering the life out of her. She's absolutely terrified," Tennant added. "I can't make her say why. Do *you* know why she's so frightened?" demanded Tennant.

"No," admitted Roger, "but I hope to, soon."

13

Strictly Unofficial

Janet and Mark arrived just inside the hour. Janet seemed to have recovered her composure completely.

Lois was in the bedroom with Tennant, who had gone in a few minutes before and who seemed to have been talking ever since. Janet looked radiant, with a high color in her cheeks, probably the glow of excitement.

Mark looked slightly peeved, doubtless because he had been so inactive.

"Well, darling?" asked Janet. "What's on?"

"The thing to accept first is that we've found the girl who paid in the money."

"What!" cried Mark.

"We can't do anything at all about it yet," Roger said. "She's been acting under compulsion and is so frightened that she doesn't know what she's doing or saying. Also she's had a visit from Masher Malone," he added, gently.

Mark said weakly: "No."

The voices continued from the other room, Lois's occasionally raised above Tennant's; it was clear that she was still refusing to explain. Roger told the others what had happened since he had left Welbeck Street and found time to explain the visit of Mrs. Sylvester Cartier and the Society of European Relief. They heard him out without comment, although Mark was scowling and Janet frowning.

"So we've got to nurse the girl to a better frame of mind," Roger said, "because she can probably give us the key to much of it, although she'll almost certainly be in some danger."

"That's fairly obvious," Janet said. "Are you going to ask for police protection for her?"

"I don't think so, yet. I think if she were to be interviewed by Abbott she'd collapse. He would be the finishing touch. For the time being I think it had better be unofficial. We won't be able to get any help from Pep, but we can use one or two of his men. Then there's this chap Tennant. That should be enough."

Mark said thoughtfully: "I rather like the sound of Tennant. I wish I'd seen him handle Malone!"

Soberly, Roger commented:

"He's made a bad enemy there. If only for the sake of revenge, Malone will come after him."

"Roger," said Janet, "I think you're making a mistake."

"Where?"

"By not telling the Yard everything. No, wait until I've finished!" she added as Roger was about to interrupt. "You've admitted that Malone is dangerous, and I think if you told them what happened here this afternoon they would arrest him."

"Even if they couldn't prove much, they would be able to keep him out of harm's way," Mark said, quickly.

"After all, they should be able to do something about what happened this morning," Janet put in. "You and Tennant can say that he actually attacked him."

Roger smiled.

"On the evidence of the three of us—always providing Lois would give evidence, which I think is doubtful, we could probably put Malone inside for a week or two, if we could find him. But he'll know that we might lodge a complaint and he'll probably keep out of the way. That apart, do we want him under charge?"

"And you're a policeman!" exclaimed Mark, shocked.

"You know as well as I do that you've often been a tower of strength because you could do things which a copper couldn't. If we put Malone inside we may not find a way of getting in touch with the higher-ups in this business, but if we let him run loose we'll be able to work through him."

"I suppose that does put a rather different light on it," Janet conceded. "All right. We'll do it your way."

"Thank you," said Roger, with mock politeness.

"What are you going to do with the girl?" Mark inquired.

"We'll take her home," said Janet.

"I see a snag if we do that," Mark said. "Roger isn't out of the wood yet and there will be Yard men watching until he is. The Yard will know that the girl is mixed up in the case and I wouldn't put it past Abbott to demand an interview with her. Besides, you've already told him that you've found who paid in the money. He'll jump to conclusions. This isn't simply an attempt to frame you, Roger. It's a pretty big show."

"You're right, of course, but where can we take her?"

"You could use my flat," Mark said, hopefully.

"Of course, the police wouldn't think of going there," Janet said, sarcastically. "*That's* no good."

"I don't see why you shouldn't go to a hotel," Roger said. "One of the glitter palaces would be a good idea."

"Nonsense!" said Janet. "Those places are all doors, and I couldn't be sure that she wouldn't run away or that someone wouldn't come and take her away. Don't you know of a small place where we could confide in the manager and put one or two of Pep Morgan's men to guard it? The more central the better, because we'd be close by. I'd stay with her, of course. There must be such a place."

"I am duly humbled," said Roger. "It's a good idea. I think I know a place where they might be able to fix you up. Mark and I would stay at Chelsea."

"The young woman might have something to say about it, as well as her young man," Mark observed.

"I think we'll be able to persuade them," said Roger. "If they come out before I'm back, introduce yourselves." He moved towards the door.

"Where are you off to?" demanded Janet.

"Only to the telephone," Roger told her.

He was back in ten minutes. No one had come from the bedroom but the voices were quieter; whether the couple had decided that it was not worth further argument, or whether they had reached an agreement, Roger could only guess. He told Janet and Mark that he had been able to make arrangements with the proprietor of the Legge Private Hotel, in Buckingham Palace Gate. It was a good-class family hotel where they would be comfortable and where, if necessary, Roger and Mark could stay for the night.

Roger went to the bedroom door and tapped.

"Just a moment," Bill Tennant called.

There was another murmur of voices before the door opened.

Apparently Lois had realized that she had made a wreck of herself and she had made-up her face quickly. She seemed to take their presence more for granted.

"I have nothing to say," she declared.

"I've tried to make her tell you everything," Tennant said, awkwardly, "but no luck."

Roger said: "It will all work out, I think. If Miss Randall doesn't feel that it's time to talk freely we'll have to accept that. Other things are more important. In the first place, both of you are in acute danger."

"Now, come off it, I—"

"Malone is a bad enemy," Roger said. "His temper won't be improved by the way you smacked him down. He has friends, and you can't handle a bunch of them in the way you handled him." He rubbed it in, conscious of the increasing anxiety in Lois Randall's eyes. "They won't stop at using knives and razors. Will they, Lois?"

Startled, she said: "No."

"How the devil do you know?" demanded Tennant.

"We've decided not to press that point," Roger told him, but he was puzzled by the girl's admission that she knew how Malone would fight. "Both of you are on Malone's list, so while he's free you'll be in danger. What I've arranged is—" he told them, briefly, of the Legge Hotel.

He expected the girl to protest but she gave the impression that she was pleased and relieved. Tennant raised the only objection.

"I don't see why I can't look after Lois. Anyhow, why are you so determined to hide her away?"

"Tennant, Lois will admit that she has impersonated my wife and as a result of it I'm in trouble at Scotland Yard—accused of accepting bribes. If anything happens to Lois, and I seriously think it will unless we take great care, one of the witnesses in my defense disappears. Why don't you take my word that the only sensible course is for you both to stay at the hotel, coming out only after dark until this affair has blown over?"

"*I'm* not going to hide from a punk like Malone!"

"When there's a chance for you to throw your weight about I'll tell you," Roger said, "but don't be obstructive now."

Again he was agreeably surprised, for Tennant shrugged his shoulders and said that he supposed Roger knew what he was talking about.

"So that's settled?" Janet asked, eagerly.

"It—it doesn't matter what you do, I can't tell you anything," Lois insisted. "I won't pretend that I wouldn't be glad to hide away, but I just can't talk." Her eyes were bright with defiance.

"Haven't we agreed that the subject's not to be discussed now?" Roger said.

"It won't be any use saying that I came with you under false pretences."

"It wouldn't enter our heads!" declared Mark, brightly and with his head on one side. "When are we moving, Roger? Now, or after dark?"

"After dark."

"Do you seriously think there is danger in daylight?" demanded Tennant.

"Oh, no," interrupted Mark. "He's going to all this trouble because he likes being melodramatic! Don't be an ass. This business is lethal and we haven't got anywhere near the bottom of it yet. Lois is in danger because she has information which might cause a lot of trouble to her so-called friends."

"I've said I'll work with you, haven't I?" Tennant was aggressive.

"That's fine!" said Roger. "All four of you go to the Legge Hotel. I'll join you as soon as I can." He had been edging towards the door casually, and with no apparent motive, but now he picked up his hat from a chair and opened the door quickly. "Tell them as much of the story as they don't know," he added. "I'll be seeing you!"

Janet stared at the closed door, then hurried across to it, pulled it open and stepped out. The door was pushed to gently as an arm slid about her waist. She gasped as Roger kissed her.

"You scared me!" she exclaimed.

"And I intended to," said Roger. "That's the kind of thing that is liable to happen in the next few days, so don't run risks. I had to slip out quickly or Mark would have wanted to come with me and I'm not happy at leaving you and Lois Randall to young Tennant on his own."

"Roger, I'm really beginning to get frightened," Janet said. "There are so many complications. Mark told me about this man Malone before."

"You've much more to worry about than him," said Roger. "Some time this evening I'm going to see one of the seven most beautiful women in the world, a Mrs. Sylvester Cartier. I haven't placed the beauty yet, she may be leading me into an elaborate trap. On the other hand, she betrayed the Refugee Society and Pickerell, so I'm taking a chance with her. This is what I wanted to tell you about. And I do *not* want Tennant or Lois to hear you tell Mark."

"What is it?" asked Janet.

"I'm going to Number 11, Bonnock House," Roger said. "I don't know where it is, I'll try to find out from Cornish—he'll try to get the information for me. If I'm not back by ten o'clock, tell

Cornish you know I was at the Mansions with Mrs. Cartier. Will you do that?"

"Of course."

"Bless you!" said Roger. He kissed her fiercely, and then hurried down the stairs. Turning at the landing and looking up he saw her standing quite still, with her eyes very bright. He felt choky as he reached the front door.

Before he stepped into the street he looked either way and by the time he reached the end of the street Janet was in the back of his mind.

He expected some sign of Malone's gang, but there was none. Perhaps Malone was still brooding over the indignity. Roger was lucky in picking up a stray taxi and sat back in the corner; he concluded that Malone was more use to him free than he would be in jail.

The complications were increasing fast, yet there was a single common factor to which he clung with eagerness and which itself troubled him: there was a hint of desperation in it. He was no longer possessed by doubts about the reason for the Masher's arrival at the "Saucy Sue." Malone had heard of Mark's visit and his gang had been summoned. There was nothing unusual about a racecourse gang haunting the East End. There was nothing surprising in Malone's activities *except* that he obviously did work for Pickerell.

Roger considered that meek and faded little man.

Pickerell had arranged the payments to the Mid-Union Bank. Lois Randall was probably a pawn, important now because he had discovered her part in the affair. Pickerell himself almost certainly knew the reason for the attempt to frame Roger.

Lois had been all right until four months ago. Her trouble had started about the same time as his, Roger's. He was still without a clue, but it was rapidly becoming clear that it was the result of something he had done or discovered the previous December. The fact that Pickerell employed Malone proved that it was a criminal conspiracy of some consequence. The fact that Malone had twice revealed himself suggested that the time for surreptitious action was past. It might mean that the culprits were getting worried—they were acting too hastily and openly, so increasing the risks.

Thanks only to Pep Morgan, the attempt to frame Roger had been no more than half successful; enough had broken open to convince even Abbott and Chatworth that their suspicions were groundless.

Pickerell's swift *volte face* and the use to which he was prepared to put Lois's evidence proved that; if Lois came again under Pickerell's direct control she would probably be prepared to swear Roger's reputation away. She was quite frightened enough to do so, but he regarded her fear as incidental, something to be dealt with when the main problem was solved.

Still pondering over the connecting links as Roger sat back in the taxi on the way to Pep Morgan's office in the Strand, he mused aloud.

"So Pickerell and Malone are working together and Joe Leech knew something which he could have betrayed. Pickerell works or worked for the Society, and Mrs. Cartier either knows something of his other activities or suspects them and decided to warn me. Which implies that she must have known of the effort to frame me."

He stopped speaking aloud when he thought of the elegant gentleman who might be Mr. Cartier. For the first time for some hours he wished that all he had to do was telephone the Yard and start inquiries into the Cartier *ménage*. By now, Abbott and Cornish would probably be investigating the activities of the family, and of the Society, but Roger would get only what information Cornish could safely pass on.

The taxi pulled up outside Pep's office.

14

Tiny Martin on the Trail

Roger paid the driver off and, walking to the lift, expected that the other taxi-driver might be telephoning Bell Street at any time. It would be wise to send one of Pep's men to his house, to take possession and receive messages.

The door of the general office was open.

Inside, a long-faced girl with lank, mousy hair was sitting in front of a typewriter on a tidy desk and looking up at one of Morgan's operatives. He was a tall, lanky man whose trilby was pushed to the back of his head and who, Roger knew, considered himself a brilliant detective. His name was Sam; the girl's was Maude. Both of them looked at Roger, the man with a grin which irritated him, and Maude expressionlessly.

"We've been waiting for you," she said; "if you'd been any later you'd have found the office shut up. We can't stay open all night."

"S'right," said Sam.

"Can't you?" asked Roger. "Pep's in hospital with a bullet in his thigh. What are you going to do? Go home and forget about it?"

"That's not true," Sam exclaimed.

"Really?" asked Maude, narrowing her red-rimmed eyes.

"If Pep's caught a packet that's different, Handsome," Sam said.

Roger said: "He has. He was working for me."

"We know," said Maude.

Roger knew that all the staff had remarkable loyalty to the twinkling little man and was relieved that he would have no further trouble in getting them to do what he wanted. Morgan employed four regular operatives and had others who would do what he required of them, legmen who specialized in more humdrum affairs. These outside agents would be brought in to carry on with the routine work of divorce cases, and the salaried operatives would be switched over to the more urgent matter.

He made arrangements quickly.

One of the operatives, called by telephone, left for the Bell Street house before Roger left the office. Roger had given him a key to the back door. Two were to be sent to the Legge Hotel. Sam was to accompany Roger. Roger would have given a lot to have had a sergeant and a plainclothes man with him, but despite Sam's mannerisms and irritating self-conceit, he was no fool. There were others who would also probably help.

From the Strand office, Roger telephoned the Yard. He asked for and this time was able to speak to Chatworth. He thought that the AC sounded less hostile than on the previous night but he gave no news of importance although he did say that Pickerell had not returned to his Lambeth flat. When the police had arrived there, they had found signs of hurried departure.

"Are you sure that he was the man who arranged for those bank credits?" Chatworth demanded.

"Yes, sir," said Roger. "But until he's found I won't be able to prove it."

"What about the girl he employed?" Chatworth asked.

"What girl?"

"Didn't you see one there?"

"There was a receptionist, yes."

"Oh," said Chatworth. "West, what were you doing at that Society office?"

"Making inquiries, sir, on my own behalf."

"Don't ignore the circumstances," Chatworth warned him.

"I'm not likely to, sir," said Roger coldly. "Good night." He replaced the receiver and looked into Sam's narrowed eyes.

"Comes to something when your own boss don't trust you," said Sam, with unexpected understanding. "They must be crazy, Handsome! Well, where are we going?"

"I've another call to make," Roger said. "You have a look in the London Street Directory for Bonnock House, will you? Cornish might not be able to tell me where it is offhand." He dialed the Yard again and spoke to Cornish, who did not know where the house was but promised to find out and to call Morgan's office. Meanwhile Maude, a cigarette drooping from her lips and a smear of ash on her soiled woolen jumper, leaned back and jerked the telephone directory from the shelf.

" 'S'matter with looking at that?" she demanded.

Roger stared, then smiled.

"Never overlook the obvious—you're right, Maude!" He turned the pages over, came to the "CAR" columns and ran his forefinger down the "Cartiers." There were several in the book and he found three entries immediately beneath each other.

Cartier, Sylvester, River Lodge, Weybridge . . . 021

Cartier, Mrs. Sylvester, River Lodge, Weybridge . . . 29

Cartier, Mrs. Sylvester, 11, Bonnock House, Hampstead . . . 54012

Maude was contemplating Roger as he closed the book.

"Got what you want?"

"Yes, thanks. It's all right, Sam," he said as the latter looked up from the Street Directory. "What's the time?" He glanced at a large clock on the wall and saw that it was a quarter to seven. He frowned.

"Ready?" Sam demanded.

"It isn't quite time to go." Roger tapped against the desk thoughtfully. "We'd better get some food, Sam, we might be working late."

"Want anything more from me?" asked Maude.

"Not tonight, thanks."

"Watch your step, Handsome," said Maude; and more ash fell from her cigarette.

As he walked down the stairs with Sam—the lift had stopped operating at half-past six—Roger found himself oddly affected by the attitude of the girl and the lanky fellow beside him. He had expected to find them gloating over the discomfiture of a Yard man; instead, their sympathy, cloaked by an air of indifference but nevertheless sincere, was heartening.

"Sam, you haven't a gun, have you?" Roger asked suddenly.

"I been thinking about one," Sam told him, earnestly. "I got one at home, Handsome; didn't think I'd need it, but if Pep's been holed maybe I ought to get it."

"I think you should," said Roger. "Where do you live?"

"Fulham Road," said Sam. "Not far. I can have some supper with my missus and tell her I'll be late, as well as pick up the rod. Does that suit you?"

Roger considered, then said: "Yes, that'll do fine. I'll be at the entrance of Bonnock House in Hampstead, at eight-fifteen. I'll meet you there."

"Okey-doke," said Sam, "I'll take a car—no limit to expenses, I hope?"

"Try not to overdo it," Roger urged, and walked towards Fleet Street.

There was a small restaurant near the Cheshire Cheese where he could get a good meal, and where he might find one or two crime reporters of the London dailies. They would probably be helpful. He did not doubt that they had heard of his suspension and, when he entered the smoke-filled ground floor room he saw two men look up at him with evident surprise.

One pushed his chair back and approached him, dabbing at his lips with a handkerchief.

"Why, hallo, West! What'll you have?" He was a middle-aged man, nearly bald and rather shabby. He was one of the best crime reporters on the Street and was reputed to have more enemies in the East End than anyone outside the police force.

"Hallo, Charlie," Roger said. "I won't have anything except some food. Is there anything good on tonight?"

"Might be in time for some roast beef," said Charlie Wray and turned to stare coldly at a younger man. He had close-cropped black hair which rose in a quiff above his forehead, a broken nose and a wide mouth with a most engaging grin. He walked with a pronounced limp. "That's if Tamperly hasn't had it all."

"Share and share alike," said Tamperly, swallowing the last of a mouthful. "I was coming to see you, Handsome. I thought—"

"I *have* seen him," said Wray, pointedly. "This is by appointment. And don't be familiar."

"I don't mind whether the *Echo* or the *Cry* gets a scoop," Roger said. "I'm too worried to take sides in a newspaper scrap. I do want some help."

"Say the word," Wray said.

"All the organization of the *Cry* will support you," promised Tamperly. "As a matter of fact, Handsome, we're running an article on you—we've whitewashed you thoroughly. Had to use the story," he added, half apologetically. "It's all over the place."

"Of course it is."

"Why waste time?" Wray demanded. They reached an empty table, Wray fetched his coffee to it and Tamperly brought the remains of a plate of roast beef and vegetables. A buxom woman came up with a bowl of soup for Roger, greeted him with a cheerful smile and told him there was a steak pudding, if he'd like it.

"You told me—" Tamperly began, indignantly.

"They're kept for the popular customers," Wray grinned.

Roger said: "I know you two would like to cut each other's throats, but could you bury the axe for half an hour? Take fifty-fifty on anything that is thrown up from this job?"

"Yes," said Wray.

"He'll try to get sixty, but I'll play ball," said Tamperly, with his engaging grin. "What's gone wrong, Handsome? I thought you were Chatworth's white-headed boy."

"I'm being framed. What I'm interested in now are two things—do either of you know anything about a man named Masher Malone with a gang in the East End?"

"I certainly do!" exclaimed Wray. "He was questioned today about Joe Leech's murder."

"Lessing was at Joe's. I wondered if it was the same job," Tamperly said.

"Did you know anything about Malone before today?" Roger asked.

Both men had heard of Malone but they had not regarded him as out of the ordinary. In their opinion, he would have his fling but one day would go too far and be put inside. Afterwards, he might gather the remnants of his gang together again but in all likelihood someone else would have taken over from him and he would fade into the background, considering himself betrayed. A big shot in his own imagination he would look back to the great days of the London gangs.

"See if you can find out more about him, will you?" Roger asked. "Next there's a man named Pickerell." He gave them Pickerell's address and the fact that he had worked for the Society of European Relief. Tamperly's grin widened and he said:

"You wouldn't want us to probe into the affairs of the Society, would you? How like you, Handsome! You don't ask for the thing you want most!"

"I haven't got to it yet, because I don't know what it is," Roger said, "and in any case I don't think the Society is connected with it. I think it's Pickerell only. He's a paid official. If you want to help me, concentrate on Malone and Pickerell."

"Nothing else?" asked Wray.

"Not now," replied Roger.

He broke off, looking across at the door, which had opened to admit an all-too-familiar figure. It was Tiny Martin, lantern-jawed and thin-lipped. Roger's heart leapt and he looked about him quickly, subconsciously thinking of getting away and fearful lest Martin had instructions to detain him. Martin, however, simply looked about the room and went to a corner table, where he called for scrambled egg and beer.

"What a stomach! But he's on your tail," Wray said. "Nasty feeling, isn't it?"

"I don't know a worse," admitted Roger. "I want to shake him off."

Wray and Tamperly exchanged glances.

Five minutes later, at exactly a quarter to eight, Roger left the room hurriedly. Before he reached the door he saw Martin get to his feet. He slammed the door behind him and hurried along a narrow passage towards the street.

Upstairs, Tamperly and Wray went for the door at the same time as Martin. Tamperly knocked against the man and apologized profusely. Martin snapped at him angrily and was halfway out when Wray, already outside, swung round with a muttered imprecation and cannoned into the sergeant, who staggered back into Tamperly.

Wray's expression was one of bewildered sorrow.

"Sorry," he said, "I've forgotten my hat. Are you all right, Tiny?"

"You'll be sorry for this!" Martin growled. He recovered his breath and hurried past them.

Roger was already in a bus heading for the West End, where taxis would probably be easier to come by. He looked out of the window and made certain that Martin had not been allowed to follow him. Wray and Tamperly would back him up in spite of their rivalry. He sat back until he reached Haymarket. He preferred to make the main journey by taxi, for he might want to leave Bonnock House in a hurry and he had no idea how far it was from the nearest station.

He found a taxi, then kept it waiting while he telephoned his home. Morgan's man answered him. There had been three telephone calls, two from Scotland Yard and one from a lady who had asked for Mrs. West and said she was her cousin. The taxi-driver named Dixon had not called.

Roger returned to the taxi, surprised that Dixon had been out for so long. It was possible that the cabby had called when the Bell Street house had been empty.

It was already dusk when the cabby found Bonnock House. One or two uncurtained windows in the big block of flats looked very bright in the gloom. He saw Sam by the drive but did not speak to him. Sam patted his pocket. One flat on the top floor of the mansions was lit up, a beacon of light which could be seen for miles. The house was a massive edifice of concrete and looked ugly and forbidding in the half-light. There was a drive-in and ample space for a taxi to park but Roger sent his man to the end of the narrow street—which was on the edge of the common—then went on foot to the house.

Number 11 was on the first floor.

The flats were obviously in the luxury class. The corridor was carpeted, the lighting was concealed, the decorations were in keeping with the general atmosphere. All the doors were painted black, the walls were of cream mottled paper which showed up clearly in the lighting immediately above it.

He rang the bell at Number 11. The door was opened by a tiny maid, neat, faded-looking and reminding him, for some reason of Mr. Pickerell.

"Is Mrs. Cartier in?" Roger asked. "My name is West."

"Yes, sir. She is expecting you." The maid stepped aside and, as Roger entered, closed the door. It might have been accidental but it seemed to Roger to close with a decided snap. He glanced sharply at the maid, but she was walking sedately towards one of the black doors at the far end of the entrance hall. She tapped on it and entered. That door, also, closed with a snap.

"I'm being a fool!" Roger muttered.

He meant that he was being foolish to let himself think that there was anything even remotely sinister about the closing of the doors and the manner of the maid, but *was* he a fool for being here? Was Sam a sufficient cover? It was nearly half past eight, and Janet was not to call the Yard until ten o'clock.

An hour and a half suddenly appeared a very long time.

The maid came out.

"Mrs. Cartier will see you now, sir."

"Mrs. Cartier," reflected Roger. A well-trained maid would have said "Madam."

But his fears and forebodings soon faded.

Mrs. Cartier rose from an easy chair in a room which set off her tall figure, perfectly gowned in black and gold. The room was pale blue, the luxurious chairs upholstered in maroon-colored mohair, the furniture Louis-Quinze, and the carpet thick and muffling his footsteps. Roger took the extended hand, resisting an absurd temptation to bow over it, then looked into the smiling face of the woman.

"I'm so glad you came," said Mrs. Cartier. "I have so much to tell you. But first, have you forgiven me for pretending to wish to see your wife when I called?"

15

Mrs. Cartier Is Helpful

"I certainly haven't forgiven you," Roger said.

"I beg your pardon."

"Mrs. Cartier, we haven't time to fence," Roger said. "I haven't forgiven you for coming to me this morning with half a story. I might easily have been murdered; a friend of mine was in fact badly wounded. Had you told me what to expect that might have been avoided." He thought that she was as shocked by his attitude as Malone had been by Tennant's unexpected versatility. "I hope you'll tell me much more than you have so far. A great deal is at stake, but you know that."

"You mean your reputation?" Mrs. Cartier's voice was soft and her smile faintly mocking.

Roger looked at her steadily.

"I really don't think that remark was worthy of you," he said.

She threw back her head and laughed.

"Come and sit down, Inspector! I shall like you, I thought from the first that I would." She lifted a carved wooden cigarette box from a table at her side and flicked a lighter into flame for him, but did not smoke herself. There was a small ashtray on the arm of the settee, kept in position by weights. She was still smiling, but there was a more sober expression in her eyes and she no longer gave the impression that she was hoping to influence him by her beauty.

"I can help you, Inspector, if you will help me."

"So it's conditional?"

"First, I want you to understand what has happened. My Society—and although you may not believe it, I have its interests very much at heart—has been used to conceal serious criminal activities. I discovered that just over a week ago. You can understand how shocked I was and how anxious to adjust the situation?"

Roger did not speak.

"I should explain that I went to the office without telling Pickerell to expect me. He was talking with the girl receptionist—so charming, don't you think?"

"I hardly noticed her."

"Then you must take my word for it, Inspector. Lois Randall is a most charming girl!" Mrs. Cartier went on. "She speaks several languages, which has made her invaluable, and her manner with those who come for help is extremely gracious. I should not like you to think badly of her."

"Why should I?" asked Roger.

"Because she has been going to your bank, calling herself your wife and making things so unpleasant for you," said Mrs. Cartier, softly.

Half-prepared for that, Roger was able to look as if the news was unexpected. He jumped to his feet and stared down at his companion.

"Please believe me. She has done all this against her will," Mrs. Cartier said earnestly. "You should be pleased to know the truth, so that you can convince your friends at Scotland Yard. Don't you think so?"

Roger said: "If this is really true—"

"Oh, it is quite true and I think I could find the—what is the word?—evidence, yes, evidence to prove it. The police are so particular about evidence, aren't they? Please sit down, Inspector, and listen to what I have to say."

Roger sat down, tapping the ash from his cigarette.

"I discovered all this because I visited the office unexpectedly and heard them talking," Mrs. Cartier declared. "Pickerell, the secretary with whom you appear to have had a difference of opinion"—she smiled her secretive smile—"and Lois Randall. She was being sent to the bank, and protested. Pickerell threatened her with some disclosure and after a while she agreed to go. I hurried out of the office and met her in the passage. I have rarely seen anyone so agitated. She was muttering to herself and when she saw me she what I believe is called 'fell through the floor.' I pretended that I knew nothing of what had happened. I was shocked because I had heard enough to make it clear that the visit to the bank was intended to jeopardize your position. I only knew you as a name, then, but I realized the gravity of the situation for you."

"Did you?" Roger asked, expressionlessly.

"I wondered how best I could warn you," went on Mrs. Cartier. "I decided not to telephone you or call to see you. I made inquiries among my friends and discovered that your wife is very active in voluntary work. That gave me an excuse to call. I was so glad that you were there yourself, but I had planned to arouse the suspicions of one or the other of you—suspicions which would take you to Welbeck Street. I hope you believe me."

"Why shouldn't I?" Roger asked.

"Is it my imagination or are you being just a little difficult?"

"It's quite a shock," Roger reminded her.

"Of course, how foolish I am!" She leaned forward and rested a hand on his arm; her long fingers were cool and soft. "I must tell you everything quickly. I realized from what I had overheard that Pickerell was not interested in the Society. I contemplated dismissing him but doubted whether that would be wholly effective. I wondered how I could help the girl and saw no way, but believed that if you discovered what was happening, you would be able to solve the problem."

"Did you indeed?" Roger said heavily.

She drew her hand away.

"Why do you disbelieve me?" Her voice was sharp and her expression angry.

Very flatly, Roger said: "All this happened a week ago, Mrs. Cartier. Had it been two days ago I could have understood the delay, but you appear to have given Pickerell good time to make his arrangements. Why did you wait for so long? And how did you learn that I was already in trouble at Scotland Yard? You've implied that you did know."

"But yes, of course," said Mrs. Cartier, her voice softer again. "I am not used to dealing with those whose life is spent in seeing the flaws in the statements of others! I will answer your second question first. I have friends, one of them on the *Echo*. I get a great deal of publicity for my Society through her and I asked her if she could get some information for me. She brought it to me yesterday, and told me that you were under suspicion and had actually been suspended. That was at dinner last night. She told me her informant was a reporter named Wray."

Roger began to think she might be telling the truth.

"I know Wray, and he certainly knew about it."

"As for the other point, Inspector—" Mrs. Cartier shrugged. "It was clear that this had been going on for several months. It did not occur to me that there was any great urgency. I wanted to make sure that I did nothing which might jeopardize the activities of the Society. I gave the matter a great deal of thought and took a long time in reaching a decision. That is the whole truth."

"I see," said Roger. "I do believe you, Mrs. Cartier."

She eyed him without speaking for some seconds and then smiled with deep satisfaction.

"Thank you," she said simply. "Now you know why I came to see you and you must realize my own problem. I need someone's assistance to make sure that the Society does not suffer because it employed a rogue. Will you help?"

"Yes," Roger said.

"I was sure you would." She pressed his hand again but quite impersonally. He wondered what nationality she had been born. "Now I will help *you*, Inspector. I've told you what you have probably known already, through Pickerell. I understand that you interviewed him this afternoon."

"Who told you that?" Roger asked sharply.

"A German doctor, a refugee who called there and saw you. He was referred to me and I have since seen him." She spoke confidently. "He is very observant. I knew he was there just before the shooting, so I asked him whether he had seen anyone else. He described a man whom I identified as you. The doctor's name is Hoysen, Dr. Karl Hoysen, once of Frankfurt-on-Oder. I will gladly arrange for you to interview him if you wish. In fact, you may have his address now."

She jumped up and went into another room, to return quickly with a small black book. She opened it and pointed at an entry; her nail was varnished pale pink.

"There, Inspector. That will satisfy you."

Roger took out a notebook and wrote the name and address of the Dutch doctor—*Karl Hoysen, the Kronprins Hostel, St. John's Wood, N.W.8.* He knew of the place, which had a good reputation.

Mrs. Cartier looked positively gay. "I promised to help you in return for your kindness. That conversation I overheard was extremely interesting. I will not ask you to trust my memory. Come!" She took his hand as he rose, then rested her hand lightly on his arm and led the way to a small library, book-lined and warm, as impressive as the lounge. There was a small period desk and, unexpectedly, a tape-recorder. She opened a cupboard beneath the bookcases and took out several tapes.

Roger watched with great hope.

"You must understand that I am aware that some of the people who come for help are not displaced persons but Russian sympathizers. For some time I have suspected that Pickerell was not all that he seemed, so I arranged for this to be installed. It was not always used, of course. I went to the office whenever suspected individuals had gone to see Pickerell. By pressing a switch outside the door, I set the machine in motion. Clever, is it not?"

"Very."

"Thank you! I must say that before hearing this recording I hadn't heard a conversation which I thought was really suspicious. Until my call a week ago I began to think I was wrong, and had misjudged Pickerell." As she spoke she was fitting the tape into the machine, then she pressed a switch.

There was a faint whirring sound as the tape began to revolve. Then softly came Pickerell's voice, alternating with Lois Randall's. Roger heard Lois protest, with a note of hysteria in her voice, saying that she would not "do it" again. Pickerell sounded suave and threatening, the girl seemed to get nearer and nearer to hysterics. Pickerell's threats—always about something he did not name—increasing. Then with a quickening tempo:

"Why, why, why?" demanded Lois, *"why must you try to ruin this man? What has he done to you?"*

Roger stiffened. Mrs. Cartier's eyes showed a repressed excitement.

"My dear, that is no business of yours," came Pickerell's voice, *"but I will tell you that a few months ago West happened upon a discovery which could do me and my friends a great deal of harm."* The man seemed to be speaking to himself and Roger could imagine Lois standing and staring at him, could picture his faded eyes and the thick lenses of his glasses. *"One day he will stumble upon the truth, and that would not do. It is one or the other of us and I do not intend that it shall be me."*

"What—what beastly work are you doing?" Lois demanded.

"That need not interest you," Pickerell said. *"What matters is that unless you do what you are told I shall deal with you severely."* His voice hardened. *"Take the money, and do exactly as you have before. Don't be foolish enough to try to betray me."*

The talking ceased. There was a rustling sound, sharp noises which might have been footsteps, and then the unmistakable banging of a door. A laugh, soft and gentle and somehow blood-curdling; Pickerell, of course.

"I must try to make sure that the bank cashier will be

amenable," Pickerell said. *"I wonder whether it is all necessary? I wonder if West will ever remember what happened on that day?"* His voice was barely audible and Roger bent down, his ear close to the tape-recorder. *"The unlucky 13th,"* Pickerell went on, and then there was a sound as if he snapped his fingers as he added in a louder, more angry voice: *"This absurd superstition!"*

The voice stopped. Mrs. Cartier switched the machine off.

Roger straightened up and looked into her eyes. His were narrowed and yet glistening. December the 13th, the unlucky 13th. He did not remember what had happened that day but his files at the Yard would surely tell him and he would surely be allowed access to them. With this tape, he could end all doubts and all suspicions.

He could have kissed the lovely Mrs. Cartier!

"You see how important it is?" she said.

"It couldn't be more important," Roger agreed. "May I have the tape?"

"Of course," said Mrs. Cartier. "Be careful with it, it's the only one." She took the tape off the machine, replaced it in its cardboard container and handed it to him. "You will keep your part of the bargain, Inspector, won't you? You will do all you can to make sure that the work of the Society is not interrupted?"

"Everything I possibly can," Roger assured her. "Is there anything else?" He smiled. "No, I'm not greedy—I'm simply trying to make sure!"

"I should not like to be a criminal with you after me," said Mrs. Cartier.

The remark was fatuous, and Roger did not quite understand why it struck a wrong note. He only knew that it did, that with the tape in his hand and the evidence he needed to clear himself there in unmistakable form, he was suddenly doubtful of this woman's sincerity. It was as if his mind had opened for a split-second, to allow him to catch a glimpse of something badly wrong, then closed up again and left him with an insistent, infuriating doubt. He did not think that he revealed it as she led him back into the other room.

The maid had been in; there was a tray with brandy and whisky, and a dish of fruit. Two large, bowl-shaped brandy glasses were warming in front of a single bar of an electric fire. The woman approached the tray.

"What will you have?"

Before Roger could answer, there was a sharp exclamation in the next room. The maid's voice rose, then Masher Malone said harshly:

"Well? Where are they?"

16

Situation Reversed

The maid did not answer.

There was no sound until a sharp report followed as if Malone had slapped her face, then the question again:

"Where are they?"

"In—in there," gasped the maid.

Roger could picture her pointing towards the door. He bent down and pushed the tape beneath a low table near the wall, then stepped to the door, getting behind it and motioning the woman towards the library. She took no notice but stood staring. It did not open immediately, but one opened elsewhere. There was an oath from Malone and a stifled scream from the maid. She had given her mistress a moment's respite by misdirecting the man.

A thud—a cry—and silence.

Roger thought tensely: "Where the devil is Sam?"

He looked round the room. There were no fire-irons, nothing at all he could use as a weapon. He didn't fancy his chances of facing Malone with the same confidence as Bill Tennant had done, even if Malone were not armed.

Doors opened and banged. Roger picked up a small upright chair and kept close to the wall. He saw the handle turn before the door was flung open.

Mrs. Cartier cried: "No, *no!*"

Roger swung the chair on the head and shoulders of the man who stepped in, but before it landed he saw that it was not Malone but a smaller man. The chair crashed on the man's shoulders and sent him sprawling, the force of the blow carried Roger forward, so that he almost ran into the overdressed figure of Malone. He saw the cosh in the man's hand as it moved downwards and caught him a paralyzing blow at the top of the arm, rose again and struck him on the side of the head. He staggered against the far wall, ears ringing, agonizing pain shooting through him.

"This way," Malone said.

Roger just heard the words but did not understand until two more men entered. The fellow whom he had hit with the chair was getting unsteadily to his feet; there was a trickle of blood on his cheek.

"We've got 'em," Malone said, with an economy of words which would have seemed remarkable at any time. He glanced at Roger and two of the men stepped to Roger's side, one striking him with a clenched fist and sending him against the wall again.

Malone stood in front of Mrs. Cartier.

His oily hair, dressed high so as to increase his stature, hardly came up to her mouth. She looked down at him, and even through the mists of pain and mortification Roger could see her draw herself up, disdainfully. Yet he believed that she was frightened, as any woman would have been by such a man in similar circumstances.

Malone spoke in his husky voice.

"Listen to me, sister. You had a tape-recorder at your office. Where is it?"

Mrs. Cartier said: "I have no idea."

Malone moved his right hand and snapped his fingers under her nose. She moved back involuntarily, and stumbled against the table. The tray of bottles shook and the whisky and brandy swayed up against the sides of the bottles.

"Don't get me wrong," Malone said. His vocabulary was grotesque in its limitations, its sprinkling of quasi-American slang. "Just say where it is, and you won't get hurt."

"I still don't understand you," she insisted.

Roger opened his mouth. "Don't—" he began.

One of the others struck him a flat-handed blow across the mouth. He felt the warm trickle of blood from his lips. He had intended to tell the woman to let Malone know but could not speak.

Malone struck Mrs. Cartier a savage blow on the right cheek, another on the left, a third and a fourth. Her head rocked from side to side, she would have fallen but for the rain of blows. Her hair spilled out from its elaborate coiffure, drooped over her eyes and face and then about her shoulders. Malone gripped a handful and tugged at it savagely, making her gasp with pain.

Roger clenched his hands, but the men held him fast.

Malone stepped back, and Mrs. Cartier brushed the hair out of her eyes. She looked older, her cheeks were red and already swollen and there was a scratch on the lid of one of her eyes.

"Tell him!" Roger cried.

He was struck again, but half-heartedly. Malone threw a careless glance over his shoulder, then looked back at Mrs. Cartier.

"The guy's got sense," he said. "Where's that machine?"

"In the other room," answered Mrs. Cartier in a voice that Roger could hardly hear. She pointed an unsteady hand towards the library and then swayed back against a chair and slumped into it, burying her face in her hands.

Malone turned to the larger of the men by the door.

"Tell him," he said. "Keep your peepers open."

"Oke," said the man. He turned and crossed the flat. Roger heard the opening of the door and at the same time realized how little noise had really been made. It was doubtful whether anyone in the adjoining flats would dream of anything out of the ordinary. The tape which meant so much lay on the floor, behind a table, where he had kicked it when he had first heard Malone's voice. Before long they would start to look for it.

Then Pickerell came in.

He walked furtively. He was not wearing glasses and his face had a hang-dog look. He averted his eyes from Mrs. Cartier, who did not look up, and went with Malone into the room where the tape-recorder was.

"Bring in the slop," Malone said.

Roger was hustled forward, unable to do or say anything to help the woman.

Malone stared at him, looking up with his narrowed, sultry eyes. Pickerell stood at one side of the tape-recorder, Malone at the other.

"Can you work this thing?" Malone demanded.

Roger said: "Yes."

"Okay. Work it."

Roger opened his mouth—and was struck across the face. He wiped a trickle of blood from his chin, then picked up a tape from the cupboard, which was open. He pressed the switch and voices came through, a conversation between Pickerell and a man who spoke in broken English.

"Is that it?" Malone asked Pickerell.

"No, that's nothing." Pickerell licked his lips.

"Try another," Malone ordered.

He took the first tape from Roger's hands and flung it against the outer wall, where it unrolled like a length of film. Roger fitted on the second with the same result; Malone flung that, too. There were perhaps two dozen tapes in the cupboard and he tried one after the other. Had Malone asked whether he knew where the tape they wanted was, Roger doubted whether he would have had the courage to keep silent. Malone's thoroughness, the slow deliberation with which he worked, helped Roger to retain sufficient moral courage to say nothing.

Time was flying. If Sam had been coming he would have raised an alarm by now. It seemed useless to hope for outside help.

The twelfth tape crashed against the wall before Malone said softly:

"You sure you'd know the one, Pickerell?"

"Of course I do," Pickerell was as frightened of the man as anyone. "The only one that could do any harm was when I gave Lois Randall instructions. It would have our voices, Masher."

"My name's Malone," the man said; "use it." To Roger: "Go on, copper."

Roger tried four more tapes.

"Why don't you find out whether—" Pickerell began.

"Close your trap!" snapped Malone. He nodded to Roger, who put on four more tapes only to take them off and see them hurled away. The carpet was covered with the shiny, worm-like tapes, and the wall was marked where they had crashed against it. There were four more left in the cupboard and Malone seemed prepared to hear them all. Pickerell opened his lips as if he were going to make another suggestion, but thought better of it. Two more tapes went the way of the others. Two more, and then there would be the inevitable questions.

Roger, his nerve steadier, was able to think more clearly. They would probably start to question Mrs. Cartier. It would be impossible to stand by and watch, he knew that he would have to speak. He knew, too, that having heard the record, he had the essential facts to work on; if he could not produce the record, Chatworth would have to take his word.

But when Malone found it he would guess what Roger had heard.

There was one tape left.

Suddenly from the outer room there came a shrill whistle, the sound which Mark had heard near the "Saucy Sue." It was clear and distinct and Roger guessed at once what it was: the gang's signal of impending danger. Malone jerked his head up and Pickerell gasped:

"What's that?"

"Pipe down," said Malone. "Someone's coming." He moved

past Roger and went towards the door. Roger could see Mrs. Cartier still slumped forward in the chair.

Voices were raised, but not loudly enough for Roger to hear the words.

Malone came back and spoke softly and with that evil glitter in his eyes.

"The busies. So you're clever, copper?" His teeth showed in an ugly sneer. "One day you won't be, you'll be kicking up the daisies. Where's that tape?"

"I don't know what—" Roger began.

"You know," said Malone, "you *know!*" He moved his right hand with bewildering swiftness, and the cosh seemed to leap into it. He hit Roger over the temple, sending him lurching over the tape-recorder, which crashed down. He did not try to pick himself up. The room was going round and the blood was pounding in his ears. He thought he heard voices and a cry of pain but could not be sure. Doors opened and closed. There was silence, until slowly he became aware of a woman sobbing. He dragged himself to his feet.

It was not Mrs. Cartier. She was on her knees beside the maid who was sitting in a chair and crying, just as Lois had cried, and her mistress was speaking to her in a soothing voice. The passage door was shut but footsteps were audible in the passage; then the bell rang. Only the three of them appeared to be left in the flat.

Mrs. Cartier looked up at him.

"Please open it," she said.

Roger went unsteadily to the door. The bell rang again as he reached it. He fumbled with the latch and pulled it open, stumbling as someone entered, as if to make sure that the door was not closed in his face. He thought he recognized the man but was not sure until a voice, for once lifted out of its habitual coldness, exclaimed:

"West! What is going on?"

It was Superintendent Abbott!

Tiny Martin and two plainsclothes men came into the room followed by the lanky Sam. Roger realized then what had happened. Pep Morgan's operative was grinning rather sheepishly. Roger knew that Sam had seen the mob come in and had guessed what they were going to do. Realizing that on his own he would be useless, he had telephoned the Yard and made the summons urgent enough to bring Abbott and these men post-haste.

Abbott put a hand on Roger's arm and led him to the bathroom. Roger felt his face being sponged, warm water soaked into his cut lips, welcome and soothing. Abbott did not speak and his bony hands were surprisingly gentle.

It was over at last.

Roger dried himself on a towel which felt as smooth as silk. There were a few pink bloodstains on it but the bleeding had almost stopped. He was sufficiently recovered to run a comb through his hair. His right eye was swollen but his left was all right and he could see Abbott clearly. The room was no longer going round and he felt all right except that his lips seemed to touch his nose, and his head ached.

"I've never been so glad to see you," he said.

"I daresay," said Abbott, his thin lips twisting in a smile. "I shouldn't try to talk too much yet." He led the way into the entrance hall and the lounge, where Mrs. Cartier was sitting in an easy chair, with coffee by her side. The maid was stretched out on the settee, her face red and swollen with crying.

Mrs. Cartier had tidied her hair. One cheek was also red and puffy and the scratch on her eyelid was lined with blood, but she looked more presentable than Roger or the maid, and she was smiling, although with more than a touch of bitterness.

"How it must hurt," she said to Roger. "Will you have some coffee?"

Roger croaked. "I don't think I could drink anything hot."

"Then some cold milk?" She rose and hurried out of the room, returning in a few seconds with a glass of cold milk.

Roger said to Abbott: "Sam called for you, did he?"

"Yes. But I think Mrs. Cartier is better able to tell me what happened."

"I will, immediately," said Mrs. Cartier. "Oh, I am so sorry that they took the tape—"

Roger snapped, his voice suddenly clear.

"Did they?" He stood up too quickly, for his head began to swim, and stepped to the cabinet beneath which he had kicked the record. He saw the cardboard container and beckoned one of the Yard men, who went down on his knees and brought it out. The tape was inside.

Mrs. Cartier said eagerly.

"That's wonderful! Now—"

Then she broke off and the others looked towards the passage door. Sam stood there ill at ease with one of Abbott's men. There was a murmur of conversation before the door opened. A plainclothes man stood aside and revealed the tall, elegant figure of Mr. Sylvester Cartier.

17

The Air Is Much Clearer

After the first shock, Cartier took the situation remarkably well. He exclaimed at the sight of his wife's puffy face and looked at Roger without understanding. Then he gripped her hands and looked into her eyes as she said:

"It is all right now, *cheri*, quite all right now."

Cartier took a blue and white spotted handkerchief from his sleeve and dabbed fastidiously at his forehead. Roger saw him closely for the first time. He was too narrow-jawed to be handsome, yet was good-looking with an excellent, almost feminine complexion. His fair hair was thin and curly, his eyes blue, his lips full and generous. There was a foppish air about him, but Roger wondered whether it was affectation.

"Now perhaps someone will be good enough to explain this remarkable visitation," said Cartier.

"*Cheri*, I should have told you something of it before," said his wife. She looked contrite and Cartier stared at her in growing bewilderment. "Perhaps you will be patient?" She looked at Abbott and added: "I would like to tell my husband what has caused this."

Cartier stepped to the tray. The fruit knives were crossed and he straightened them, then picked up an apple and toyed with it.

"I should like to know it myself," Abbott said drily. The man was positively human and Roger looked at him, surprised by this revelation, puzzled also by something else in his manner.

"Then please listen," said Mrs. Cartier.

Roger liked her telling of the story, touching on all she had told him and elaborating only those details which needed fuller explanation. She mentioned her visit to Bell Street and explained that she had seen Roger waiting at the end of Welbeck Street and had hurried off to arrange for this visit. She admitted that she and her husband had quarrelled at Welbeck Street, and she made it clear that because of his antagonism to her interest in the Society she had hesitated to take him into her confidence. She gave Roger the impression that the issue would have to be settled between them and that she was prepared to make concessions. Her eyes seemed to caress the man.

Then she told them what had happened at the flat.

Tiny Martin, probably the most proficient shorthand-writer at the Yard, took everything down, occasionally forced to write so fast that his pencil seemed to slide across the page of his note-book.

"I would have refused to answer but the Inspector told me to," Mrs. Cartier finished.

"I should think he did!" exclaimed Cartier. "I've never heard anything so wicked." He broke off, put the apple down, stared at Roger and then went on: "Had you any idea what Pickerell was doing before? If you did, you should have advised me."

"I hadn't the faintest idea," Roger told him.

"Are you sure?"

"I don't think that the Inspector would lie about it, Sylvester," said Mrs. Cartier. "It is clearly evident that as he was being victimized, he would hardly know." She looked at Abbott. "The wrong can be righted, I hope."

Abbott so far forgot himself as to smile.

"Yes," he said. "And it will be."

Roger no longer noticed his swollen lips or puffy eye. Malone had receded, even the "unlucky 13th" did not matter. He was in the clear, and Chatworth would admit it as freely as Abbott.

Roger left Bonnock House with Abbott, half an hour later,

when the flat had been scoured for finger-prints: there would be plenty of Malone's on the fragments of the tapes, which were carefully collected and put in a big bag which the maid, now much more herself, brought from the kitchen. Cartier revealed himself to be acute and shrewd by his questions to Abbott, but he gave the impression that the main issue would have to be decided between him and his wife.

Although it was barely half past nine, Roger telephoned the Legge Hotel to find that Janet and the others were there. He told an excited Janet what had happened, and rang off. He frowned, thinking of Lois and wondering whether the time had come to tell the Yard all that he knew about her. He thought it had, but as he left the flats with Abbott he felt undecided.

Sam had gone ahead.

The moon was rising and casting a faint grey light about the heath and the large houses and mansion flats bordering it. It shone dully on the three police cars outside.

The thought of the taxi-driver who should have telephoned Bell Street by now entered Roger's mind. He missed a step, and Abbott asked:

"What is it, West?"

"I ought to telephone my house," Roger said.

"You can do that from the Yard," said Abbott. "I called Sir Guy before I left and I expect he will be there ahead of us. I don't want to keep him waiting."

At the Yard, Abbott went to the AC's office ahead, and Roger went into his own. It was dark and there was a smell of shag: Eddie Day's tobacco.

Morgan's man answered his telephone call to Bell Street.

"Have you had any calls?" Roger asked.

"No, it's been all quiet," the man replied. "Think there's any need for me to stay, Mr. West?"

"Yes," said Roger. "But there's no reason why you shouldn't go to bed in the room with a telephone."

"If you say so," the man said.

Roger replaced the receiver, then called the London Hospital.

He was given a good report on Pep Morgan. At last he walked along to Chatworth's office. One or two men passed, staring in surprise, and one of them asked him what he had done to his face.

Roger grinned painfully. Tobacco smoke stung his lips and he knew that he was a fool to smoke but could not bring himself to throw the cigarette away. He tapped on Chatworth's door and was bidden to enter.

Chatworth was sitting back in his big chair, Abbott standing like a statue beside him; the tape-recorder in Chatworth's office was near his hand, a tape—*the* tape—was in front of Chatworth.

"Hallo, West," said the AC. "You've had a nasty time, I hear. Sit down." Roger did so. "Anyway, the air is much clearer," said Chatworth.

"Thank you, sir," Roger said. It was difficult to speak and his words were inclined to run into one another.

Chatworth tapped the tape.

"I propose to take this as conclusive," he said. "I must admit I'm bewildered." For Chatworth that was a great admission. "I could not bring myself to believe that anyone would go to such lengths to frame you." He hesitated, his round face somber. "It remains hardly credible."

"I suppose not, sir," mumbled Roger. *Was* he still doubtful? He decided that it was not a question of doubt but of sheer bewilderment, and he felt better although the mood of exhilaration had passed. "Have you heard about the unlucky 13th?"

"Yes." Chatworth indicated two manila folders on his desk. "Here are your reports for December 13th—it can only be the 13th of December."

"Of course," said Roger, his heart beating faster. "Have you looked through them?"

"I'm leaving it to you," said Chatworth. "But are you up to it just now?"

"I ought to try," Roger said. He pulled his chair nearer the desk, as the folders were pushed towards him. "Was there any other indication about my alleged misdemeanors?" The question sounded absurdly formal. He knew that the evidence of the bank pass-book must have seemed conclusive enough and yet there was a lingering doubt.

"Yes," Chatworth answered. "There were statements that you had conspired with the man Malone, to warn him if action were to be taken against him."

"Who made the statements?"

"Joe Leech," said Chatworth. "There were other things which we won't worry about now. If I were you I would go home and get some sleep. You'll feel much fresher tomorrow. But if you insist on looking through those files—"

"I would like to."

Ten minutes later, puzzled and frustrated, he pushed them away. There was nothing to give him any idea why he had been victimized because of a discovery made on December 13th. Certainly nothing he had put in his reports was important enough to have worried Pickerell so much. The only thing of importance on the day had been a visit to a house in Battersea, where a man had murdered his wife. It had been a miserable affair, brightened only by the solicitor who had taken on the murderer's defense. He sat back after he had told Chatworth so and the glimmering of an idea entered his mind, only to fade again. It reminded him of his flash of doubt concerning Antoinette Cartier. It faded as swiftly but made him feel uncertain and a little irritable. His eyes felt as if they were filled with grit and his tongue was like a plum against his lips.

"I spent most of the day clearing up the Battersea murder," he said. "The man Cox had murdered his wife and buried her beneath the kitchen floor of a hovel in Battersea. Oliphant looked in while I was at the house. The other things were trivial, sir, just detail."

"Get off home," Chatworth said. "You're too tired to think clearly." He rounded the desk and held out his hand. "Your suspension is lifted, West." His handclasp was very firm.

"Thank you, sir," said Roger, stiffly.

"And I'm also sorry," said Abbott, when they were walking

along the passage outside. "I had my job to do, you know that. I thought there was no doubt at all."

Roger smiled, painfully. "If there was even more evidence than I've yet heard, I can't blame you."

"I should have kept an open mind," Abbott said. "I tried to trap you, West—I told you as nearly as I could that I was coming to see you that afternoon, then I sent Martin to shadow you. I expected you to make a call on the way." The Superintendent broke off. Roger could understand how difficult he found it to make this admission.

"Forget it," said Roger. "There is one thing."

"Yes?"

"Why didn't you detain me?"

Abbott shrugged. "We wanted to give you plenty of rope."

Roger said: "And you've no idea what I was supposed to be hiding?"

"None at all. I hoped we would get information from Leech." They were walking down the steps of the Yard, then, towards the Embankment; the moon was shimmering on the sluggish Thames and the dark silhouettes of barges were moving down river. One hooted, mournfully. A car-horn sounded not far away and a lorry clattered along the Embankment, a ghostly thing with its faint lights. "You have no idea where to find Malone, I suppose?"

"No," said Roger. "I only wish I had!"

"I'll drive you home," said Abbott.

"Not home—Buckingham Palace Gate," Roger said, and then stopped abruptly, remembering Lois; he had quite forgotten her while he had been with Chatworth. His mind was too clouded, he should not have tried to think, it only gave him a headache and depressed him. He went on: "There's one other thing you should know. I've got the girl who helped Pickerell." Hastily, he went on: "Oh, I haven't kidnapped her! She is willing enough to take help, but she won't make any statement. Pickerell was blackmailing her. I think it would be a mistake to interview her officially."

Abbott did not answer immediately.

"She might be able to give us a line if she's treated well," Roger went on. "But I believe she's so frightened of the police that she would stay dumb."

Abbott gave a thin laugh; with a shock, Roger realized that he had never heard the Superintendent laugh before.

"We owe you *some* licence," Abbott said.

He did not even ask where Lois Randall was staying. Nor did he get out of the car outside the hotel, but wished Roger good night and then drove off, after promising to send men to help guard the hotel. Roger watched the rear lights fade into the gray pallor cast by the moon, then stepped towards the front door. One of Morgan's men said: "Good night, Mr. West." There was no night porter and he had no key, but Legge, a rotund, jolly individual, came to the door promptly. After he drew back bolts there was a noise of chains being moved; Legge was taking no chances.

Roger felt a twinge of alarm.

"Is everything all right?"

"Why, yes, Mr. West," said Legge. "Why shouldn't it be? I believe your wife is in the upstairs lounge." The light in the hall revealed his wide smile.

"*Roger!*" called Janet. She came to the head of the stairs and into his arms. "Darling, I get the most horrible ideas these days, I'm as touchy as—" she broke off, for he winced when she kissed him. "Roger, what is it?"

"I—er—I banged into a door," mumbled Roger.

"I don't believe it!"

When she saw his face she refused to allow him to talk, although Mark and young Tennant, also in the lounge, were obviously disappointed. Roger said enough to make them realise that he had had another encounter with Malone.

Nothing was clear to him. He did not even realise that Janet sent a lugubrious Mark to an all-night chemist near Victoria Station for some zinc ointment to put on his lips. When he undressed his limbs felt like lead, his head throbbed. He was soothed by Janet, but half-asleep when the salve was rubbed in. Janet's face was outlined against the electric light, which she had covered with a handkerchief to save his eyes from glare. It made her hair look radiant and her face soft and lovely.

When he woke it was nearly ten o'clock.

Janet, in a dressing-gown, came in from the bathroom and the opening door disturbed him. He opened one eye; the other was stuck. He heard her exclaim. He tried to speak but his lips were far too swollen. Only after he had managed to swallow a cup of lukewarm tea and eat some porridge did he feel better in himself. Even then he had to admit that he would not be much good that day.

After twelve o'clock Janet brought in a lotion to reduce the swelling at his eye, which was badly discolored, and his lips. Abbott telephoned to tell him not to come in. Later, he sent the two five pound notes from the £1,000 which Morgan had found in his bedroom to the Yard, with a note asking if they could be traced; he might learn something from them.

He kept going over the case of the man Cox, who had murdered his wife and buried her beneath the floorboards of the kitchen.

He persuaded Janet to let him send for the complete file of the December 13th case and spent the afternoon brooding over it. It was sordid, unpleasant and unremarkable. The motive had been greed: the man's wife had been on bad terms with her husband and had hoarded several hundred pounds in the house. Relatives had first suspected that something had happened to her and the case had followed its usual course—once suspicions were aroused, and the body found, it had been a mere matter of routine. There seemed no possible mistake, certainly nothing which had not been disclosed during the course of the investigation.

Mark Lessing and Bill Tennant went out during the afternoon, too restless to stay indoors. Lois Randall stayed in; during tea, she seemed unable to remove her gaze from Roger's battered face.

Abbott, showing a solicitude quite out of character, telephoned to say that there was no trace of Malone, who had left his home in Stepney, nor of his men, nor of Pickerell. There was nothing to report from the office of the Displaced Persons' Society except—Abbott seemed ill at ease when he admitted this—that the offices had not been guarded all the time after the fire and there was evidence that Malone had visited the place and discovered the tape-recorder. The overeagerness of Cornish doubtless explained the lapse, for the office should have been watched. It was reasonably obvious that Roger had been seen to go to Mrs. Cartier's flat, and that Malone or Pickerell had guessed it was her tape-recorder.

In spite of the quiet day, Roger was glad enough to get to bed just after eleven o'clock. His face was much better and Janet said, optimistically, that the scars would hardly be noticeable in the morning.

To their mutual surprise she was right. The lotion had performed miracles and his lips had healed, although he still found it difficult to eat or drink anything hot.

He went round to the Yard and saw Chatworth and Abbott, as well as an enthusiastic Cornish—his eagerness unaffected by the slip at the Society's office, and an "I-told-you-so-Handsome" Eddie Day, as well as a number of sheepish individuals who took the opportunity to say that they had always been sure it would all prove a mistake. Chatworth gave him chapter and verse of the "case" against him, including reports that he had been to visit Malone (until then hardly known to the Yard). Joe Leech had given categorical evidence that Malone had boasted that he had West in his pocket. Cornish had assessed Malone merely as a nuisance, before his transfer from the Division to the Yard, and the Division had continued to make that grievous mistake.

There was a report on the two fivers. Leech's fingerprints were on them. Leech had often been suspected of handling stolen money.

On two occasions, in the past month Roger had gone to the East End on inquiries which had given him an opportunity to see

Malone. On both occasions Malone had come out of the house he had visited after he had gone. Tiny Martin and Abbott had seen that for themselves.

"Oh, there was a case all right," Roger said to Janet, Mark and Tennant. "Apparently Leech told Abbott that he had heard that Malone was bringing a packet of money to Bell Street and that he was going to put it in the bedroom. Thanks to Winnie Marchant, Pep Morgan had learned of it. The only established fact is that Leech was bribed to lie to Abbott and then killed in case Mark forced the truth out of him."

"At least I've helped a bit," Mark said.

"Do you think that's certain?" Janet asked. "I mean why Leech was killed?"

"Malone was afraid he would crack under Mark's interrogation," Roger said. "Malone knew Leech well—so did most people in the East End. We at the Yard had rarely found him to lie to us. He's been a reliable squealer, otherwise Chatworth wouldn't have acted as he did. But when Leech told a categorical story it made 'em sit up and take notice."

"We know one or two other things," Mark pointed out, sitting back in a winged armchair, gaily loose-covered, his austere face set in concentration. Tennant looked at him curiously. "Pickerell is not even in authority over Malone, but Malone isn't running the whole show. Whoever is, knows him." He startled Tennant by beaming at him. "Any ideas?"

"Never was an ideas man," declared Tennant. When Roger and Janet laughed, he went on: "What's so funny?"

"Not funny—refreshing," Janet hastily rejoined. "It's a relief to meet a man who doesn't pretend that he knows everything! I suppose"—she looked very thoughtful—"Lois didn't say anything that might help?"

"Nothing at all. When I discovered how badly she was feeling I had the shock of my life." Tennant stood up and stepped restlessly across the room. "This doing nothing is getting me down," he went on. "If I could get at the beggars and put the fear of death into them it wouldn't be so bad." He was troubled as well as impatient. "If only I knew why Lois is so scared! I can't understand it at all. She's got no close relatives, and as far as I know she hasn't any close friends. But if Pickerell was blackmailing her, she must have—" he broke off.

"How long have you known her?" asked Roger.

"Just over a year. She was running a mobile canteen for the NAAFI." Tennant ran a hand over his curly hair. "She seemed as happy as could be."

"What part of London?" Janet asked.

"Battersea," Tennant answered.

Roger sat up. "Battersea? Are you sure?"

"Roger, you've got Battersea on the brain because you were there on December 13th," Mark declared.

"Did Lois live in Battersea?" Roger inquired.

"At the time, yes," said Tennant, coloring. "As a matter of fact, I persuaded her to leave her digs—oh, it would be about six months ago now. I didn't like the people she lodged with. He was a pretty nasty customer and he and his wife were always rowing. It's a district where neighbors don't worry about what happens in the house next door. She moved to the flat at St. John's Wood, and I think she likes it better." He frowned, for Roger was eyeing him with a peculiar expression. "Well, what have I said wrong now?"

"Nothing," Roger assured him, "nothing at all." His voice was strained. "Did she lodge at a house in New Street?"

Tennant gaped. "Why, yes, how did you know?"

"Was the man's name Cox—Benny Cox?"

"Yes! What do you know about him?"

Roger spoke very gently, Mark's eyes were startled, Janet stood up quickly, obviously guessing what was coming.

"Benny Cox was hanged for the murder of his wife," said Roger in the same strained voice. "I was at New Street on December 13th, looking around the house. That can't be simply a coincidence!"

18

One Mystery Solved

"Yes," said Lois. "I knew."

She stood by the dressing-table of the room which she shared with Janet. She had been sitting reading and had not undressed. Her hair was untidy and she had not made up—she looked pale and in her eyes was the familiar gaunt, distraught look. Her hands were clenched. The book she had been reading was on the floor by her feet.

In the other room, probably close to the door, were Mark and Tennant. Janet sat at the foot of the bed.

"You mean you knew that Mrs. Cox had been murdered," Roger said.

"Yes."

"Listen, Lois," said Roger. "I've tried to help you and I've given you ample time to think this over. I've used my influence at Scotland Yard to save you from being officially questioned, all this on the assumption that there was a strictly personal reason why Pickerell and Malone were able to force you to work for them."

"I didn't say it was personal," said Lois.

As he looked at the girl, Roger wondered whether he would not have been wiser to have left this to Mark; probably she was more frightened of him because he was a policeman.

"What Roger means," Janet said, "is that since he knows this he can't stop the other police from questioning you much longer.

You'd be much wiser to tell him what's worrying you. He'll help, you know, and the police aren't ogres. They'll take into account the fact that you've had such a bad time."

"It doesn't matter," Lois said.

"I don't want to have to send for a colleague," Roger said. "If you tell me the whole truth I'll do everything I can to make sure that they don't hear every detail. I really shouldn't make such an offer, but I'll keep my word if you'll tell me what you know."

She said: "You won't. You're like all policemen, as soon as I've told you, you'll use it against me." She stopped, drawing in a deep breath.

"You think I'll charge you," Roger said. "I won't. I'll give you this firm undertaking: if what you tell me means that you ought to be charged and arrested, I'll have Mark Lessing and Bill Tennant get you away from here."

The girl's eyes were clouded as she looked at him, but Roger thought there was a glimmer of expression in them, as if hope were being reborn.

"I—I don't believe you," she said, but her tone suggested that she wanted to.

"You should, dear," Janet said.

Lois swung round on Roger.

"I knew you'd worm it out of me. I knew someone would have to know, but—oh, don't lie to me! Don't try to pretend that it doesn't matter, that the police won't take any action. Let me know the worst. I can't bear the suspense any longer!"

Roger could hardly wait for her to go on:

"I—I've worked for Malone," she said. "I knew he was a thief, and dealt in stolen goods. Do you see that?" She held up her hand, where the single diamond scintillated in the bright light. Her face was drawn and almost haggard. "I always said it was my mother's. It wasn't, I stole it from a shop after a fire. I don't know what came over me, I—"

She paused, then went on in a steadier voice:

"But what's the use of lying? The jeweler's shop had caught fire. I happened to be passing, and this was almost at my feet. I picked it up and put it on. The fire engines were making a terrible noise, there were flares over the building, it was a devil's light and all the fire in the world seemed to be in that diamond. I told myself that I would give it up the next day, that I only wanted to wear it for a few hours, but I knew I was lying to myself, I knew I meant to keep it!"

She paused again but neither of the others interrupted her.

She went on fiercely: "I didn't know that a man had seen me. It was Benny Cox, the man who owned the house where I lodged. He didn't tell me at first but a few days afterwards he started admiring the ring, and I realized that he knew where I'd got it. I thought he meant to try to bargain for his silence—he was a beast of a man, always sleeping with different women. Instead, he told Malone."

"*Ah!*" exclaimed Roger.

She did not seem to hear him.

"Cox worked for Malone although I didn't know it then. Malone came to see me. You—you know what he's like. He frightened me. I was so scared that I don't think I could have refused him anything. He didn't stay long, just said that if I wanted nothing said about the diamond I must do whatever Benny Cox told me to. I'd got the job with the Displaced Persons' Society, and we have regular collections of jewelry for the funds. It was easy to keep valuables at the office. Benny was always bringing me things, sometimes jewelery wrapped up in paper, sometimes furs, oh, dozens, hundreds of different things! I hid them among our collection of cheap jewelery. There was always another helper with me, of course, and several times—on Benny's instructions—I handed a trinket to the police, to make out that I was being honest. The only thing I'd taken was the diamond, I didn't get paid for anything I did. I stayed at New Street and Benny made no approaches to me. He wouldn't talk about Malone although I knew he worked for him. Then a year ago, Malone came again. He told me that someone was looking for a girl who could speak languages. I know French, Dutch and Flemish, that's why I got the job. Pickerell was the manager, but I didn't know for a long time that he was also involved. I thought it was a spy organization, but soon I found that it wasn't. I had to take messages to different people and sometimes to Malone. I knew that there was a lot of stealing. I had to take packages to different men, sometimes to jewelers. I realized that the Society was used as a distributing office. Mrs. Cartier didn't know, only Pickerell did.

"Then I met Bill," Lois went on simply. "Soon I moved away from Battersea and no one raised any objections. It—it became just part of ordinary business. I didn't think of it as crime for months on end, until—until they started to send me with the money to your bank. They didn't tell me what I was really doing, you were known only as "West" and I didn't realize that you were a policeman until Malone came one day and I overheard what he said to Pickerell. But—what *could* I do?"

"Nothing," Roger said, quietly.

She stared at him. "Nothing? You have the nerve to stand there and say 'nothing'! I could have told you what was happening, gone to the police-station and made them understand it, I shouldn't have cared what happened to me. Sometimes I thought that it would be a relief to get it all over and to come out of prison after serving my sentence knowing that there was nothing hanging over my head. But there was Bill. And I couldn't screw myself up to it, I just went on and on, until that day when you came in."

She fumbled with her handbag and to Roger's surprise she took out a cigarette-case. Her fingers were trembling. He saw several little tablets in the case—or rather, their reflection in the mirror; Janet could not see them.

Roger snapped: "Don't be a fool!"

She swung away, making Janet stumble, and put her hand to her lips, but Roger knocked it away. The tablets flew across the room and struck against the far wall. Lois stood staring at him, wide-eyed.

"I—I don't want to live!" she gasped.

Roger was looking into her face when the door burst open and Tennant strode in.

"What are you doing to her?" he demanded in a harsh voice. "You told me you wouldn't do anything."

Roger said, without looking over his shoulder:

"She has tried to kill herself because she doesn't think you'll be interested in her when you know that she has mixed with thieves and rogues."

"I don't care what she's done!" Tennant rasped.

"Do you mean that?" demanded Roger.

"Of course I mean it."

Janet caught Roger's eye. He squeezed Lois's shoulders and spoke without smiling.

"If the worst comes to the worst you might be sent to prison for six months. By telling everything you know, you'll almost certainly be given a suspended sentence, and you'll have paid for what you've done by giving information about the others. And you haven't been so very wicked, you know."

Then he turned and left her. Janet was already at the door and Mark in the other room. Janet closed the door firmly as Tennant asked:

"Lois darling, what *is* it all about?"

"That's exactly what I want to know," said Mark, eagerly. "What is it all about, Roger?"

Roger told him, glad of the opportunity of going over it again. He could see how carefully the situation had been built up, how the weight of Lois's conscience had worsened her plight in every way and encouraged her to play into Malone's hands. He had deliberately made comparatively light of it, believing that she had suffered enough already. He did not think she would hesitate to make a full confession now, but when he finished, Mark put into words one of the thoughts which weighed heaviest on his mind.

"Malone knows what she can do and won't let her stay free for long without making a big effort to get her."

"That's the risk," admitted Roger.

Janet said: "The best place for her is in a police-station. *I* won't be happy until she's in one."

"I told Tennant so this afternoon, and I think she'll be amenable," Roger said. "When she's told him all about it, she'll be a different girl. I don't think he'll let her or us down." After a pause, he went on: "At least, we're making some progress. I certainly missed something at New Street, Battersea: I didn't discover that Benny Cox was one of Malone's gang, which was bad."

"Do you think that's the only reason they tried to frame you?" Mark sounded incredulous.

"It's probably one of them," Roger said. "Friday the 13th. Pickerell sounded annoyed with superstition. I thought, when I first heard that record, that it meant he himself was superstitious, but I'm beginning to wonder if someone else didn't give him his instructions, someone who was influenced by the 13th. The thing is, if I had seen a connection between Cox and Malone I would have been after Malone very quickly. We've always assumed that Cox killed his wife for her money, but supposing she had discovered what he was doing, supposing New Street was used for storing stolen goods and Mrs. Cox threatened to tell the police?" Roger frowned. "Cox was a miserable little brute. I can't imagine him going through the trial and letting himself be hanged, if by squealing on Malone he might have saved his life."

"I see what you mean," said Mark.

"On the other hand, he may have killed her and, knowing that he couldn't save himself no matter what he did, just let things go," Roger went on. "He acted dumb all the time. I once thought that the defense might try to prove insanity, Oliphant hinted at it once or twice, but Oliphant's a good enough lawyer to know whether the plea would have a chance of success. Cox hardly said a word once he was caught, it seemed as if the shock was too much for him. Dull-witted," he added, "*very* dull-witted." His voice rose. "*Too* dull-witted?"

"What the deuce are you getting at?" demanded Mark.

Roger said, softly: "I'm wondering if Cox was drugged before we caught him, and whether that made him seem so dull?"

19

Lois's Whole Story

Mark said dubiously that it was a possibility, but wasn't Roger allowing his imagination to run away with him? Roger went into the other room and took out the Cox case files. He turned up the medical reports and scanned them. Three doctors had examined the man, one for the police, two for the defence. They were unanimous in saying that Cox had been a person of low mentality, on the verge of subnormality. The police doctor said that there was no doubt at all that he knew what he was doing and he was fully responsible for his actions. Obviously medical opinion for the defense had not really thought it possible to prove otherwise, and so the defence, in the hands of Oliphant, had not tried to sway the jury on the grounds of insanity.

"Reflexes, dull," Roger read, "pulse below normal, pupils enlarged . . ." "A man who had been given one of the depressant drugs might be in that state for months after his last dose."

"Well?" asked Mark, after nearly half an hour's silence. "Have you found anything?"

Roger seemed to be thinking of something else.

"Er—no," he said. "That is—no, it *can't* be!"

"How brightly he goes on," drawled Mark.

"Do be quiet," said Janet.

Roger thought again of Friday the 13th.

The sordid little house, the floorboards, the nauseating smell, the "straightforward" murder and the dull-witted Cox. He remembered him at the police-station awaiting the second hearing at the police court; he had been remanded for eight days at the first.

"I just can't credit it!" he exclaimed, standing up and pushing his chair back.

Mark shrugged his shoulders and said in sepulchral tones:

"The great policeman is slowly going insane."

Janet said:

"Can we help, Roger?"

"No," said Roger. "No. That is—I was at New Street collecting all the paraphernalia of evidence. The camera-work was done, and the fingerprints. I'd found the hammer which Cox used. There were bloodstains on the wood. He hadn't cleaned it properly, and it certainly caused the wounds in his wife's head. In short, all the evidence was there. I was going off, feeling fully satisfied although it was a nasty case—"

He paused.

Mark no longer acted the fool, but eyed him intently. The voices came from the other room in a steady ripple.

"A taxi drew up outside," Roger said. "Oliphant came out. Oliphant," he repeated, softly. "He said that he had been asked to act for Benny Cox." He leaned back in his chair with his eyes closed. He saw the portly solicitor, Mortimer Oliphant, a well-known lawyer who frequently acted for poorer criminals. He was ambitious and took on difficult jobs which a less forceful solicitor would have refused. He worked for the *Poor Person's Legal Society* and was one of its brighter members.

Mortimer Oliphant had a man at court regularly, and if a case appeared particularly tricky, or whenever there seemed to be the slightest chance of pulling off an odds-against case, he would volunteer to take it. He briefed young barristers who usually did well. His reputation was excellent and he often managed to win a case which the police thought was a foregone conviction. A man of middle-age, he had a large private income. He always claimed that he specialized in criminal cases because he liked the excitement of matching his wits against the police.

Roger remembered the smile on Oliphant's face when he had squeezed along the narrow passage and seen Roger in Cox's kitchen. He had pulled a wry face and said that he hoped it wasn't necessary to stay in that atmosphere for long. Roger had not thought twice about his arrival, for he had guessed why he had come.

"I'm going to look after Benny Cox," Oliphant had stated.

Roger remembered smiling. "You've backed a loser this time!"

"Oh, I don't know," Oliphant had said. "I always enjoy a few rounds with you. You don't mind if I look round?"

Roger remembered admiring his thoroughness. Few solicitors would have taken the trouble to come to the scene of the crime. He had thought nothing of it even when he had read through his report for the day—"*Oliphant saw me at New Street and said that he was going to handle Cox's defence.*" He had not troubled to question that, for it was the kind of thing that Oliphant did. Also, he came to the Yard often and asked for information. Being a likeable man one somehow always gave him what he wanted. Roger vaguely remembered another thing; that Oliphant had been called to the telephone one day at the Yard.

"You shouldn't call me here," he had rebuked the caller. "What is it you want, Mal—?"

That "Mal" could have been short for Malone.

"Oliphant," said Mark, quietly. "Didn't you say that he handled Cox's defence?"

Janet answered for Roger. "Yes."

"You think—" Mark began, but his voice trailed off.

"I can't think of anything else which might have made Malone and his leaders fear that I might have been given an inkling of what was going on," Roger said. "Oliphant doesn't often visit the scene of the crime—he usually gets to the case when it's too late to be useful—but he was very quick this time. Supposing he was briefed by Malone or whoever Malone is working for? Supposing he realized afterwards that his eagerness might have been suspect? He would tell his client, of course.

The client is superstitious. It happened on the 13th—'one of these days West is bound to see something funny in it, we'll have to make sure that he can't do any harm.' It would answer everything," Roger said.

"Would Oliphant let anyone go for you, Roger?" Mark asked. He knew the solicitor well and obviously found the suspicions hard to believe.

"He might," said Roger. "He might even have thought that I was keeping something up my sleeve. I was feeling in a good mood that morning and made one or two cracks, the kind that come out when everything has gone well. Oliphant might have misread my attitude. He might have discussed it with his client. The framing was clever. Not too obvious, just enough to make sure that Chatworth would have to take notice of it. Whoever planned it knew Leech's reputation with us. Malone might have known everything else, but he couldn't have known that we relied so much on Leech. Oliphant would know that. I wonder—" he stood up slowly—"I wonder who the legal adviser to the Society of European Relief is? We'd better phone the Yard and find out."

"I'll do it," said Mark, promptly.

Oliphant loomed so much in Roger's mind that he did not notice the louder note of Tennant's voice in the next room.

The door opened and Tennant strode out, holding Lois by the hand, a Lois who seemed much more at peace.

"It's all right!" declared Tennant.

"What's all right?"

"I've fixed it—I mean, we've fixed it," declared Tennant. "She's told me everything. There's no need for you to question her again, I've got it all written down. You want the names of the people she went to see, don't you?"

"I certainly do," said Roger.

"I knew you would," said Tennant. "She's remembered a dozen—they're all on the list, together with the gist of what she told you." He put a small notebook in front of Roger and beamed widely. "All written in ink and Lois has signed it. But," he added with a quick frown, "you've got to keep your side of the bargain. I don't know much about the law but I do know there's such a thing as Queen's Evidence. If this isn't Queen's Evidence, I don't know what is!"

Roger said: "Yes, you're right." He looked at Lois reassuringly. "It will all work out well. We're far more interested in finding these people and stopping their crimes than in you."

Tears were close to Lois's eyes.

Before he looked at the list, Roger said:

"There's just one thing. While Malone is free—"

"I've talked to her about that," Tennant said. "This afternoon you said the safest place for her would be a police-cell, didn't you? Malone can't get into one of those! Well, Lois agrees!"

Lois nodded.

"You couldn't have made a wiser decision," said Roger.

He did not know how Tennant had made the girl feel that it was safe to trust the police. She did not protest, nor did she try to stipulate any conditions.

Before going to Mark, who was still on the phone to the Yard, and taking over from him, he ran his eye down the list of names and addresses which Lois had dictated to Tennant, thinking that it would probably be enough to break the case wide open. The last entry but one made him start and look up eagerly into her eyes.

"Oliphant—Mortimer Oliphant, at Cheyne Walk, Chelsea?"

"Yes," said Lois, quietly.

"Did you ever go there with stolen jewels?"

"No, only with messages about men whom Pickerell knew. He was the Society's legal adviser, but these weren't Society problems. Pickerell always saw him alone." She hesitated. "I rather liked Mr. Oliphant. He was always very friendly."

"Oh, yes, he would be," Roger said. "He would be very friendly indeed!"

Mark came back like a man with good tidings, but suddenly deflated when he learned that Lois had already given the information.

Roger felt on edge, in spite of the way the case was shaping. He wanted to see Oliphant, to report his discoveries, and to make sure that Lois was absolutely safe. He realized that few bad men had made such an impression on him as Malone. He did not feel sure that the short journey to the Yard could be negotiated safely and he went out, to see Pep Morgan's men and the two police who were watching the hotel. They assured him that nothing suspicious had happened. He sent one of the police back to the Yard to get a car.

The policeman took the wheel.

Tennant had been persuaded, with some difficulty, to stay behind. Mark had accepted the inevitable with commendable fortitude, but Janet would have her hands full with the two men.

Lois was very quiet; at least she did not seem to share any of his fears.

As they turned into Parliament Square, he said:

"We won't be long, now."

Lois spoke quietly, unexpectedly using his first name.

"Roger, I—don't know how to thank you. Those tablets were powerful."

"Forget it," Roger said. "I have." As he spoke he realized what a fool he was, how the spectre of Malone and the dazzling prospect of outwitting Oliphant had driven other thoughts from his mind. "That is, I'd forgotten you were going to take them," he amended hastily. "Where did you get them from, Lois?"

"Pickerell," she said.

"You know what's in them?"

"Yes," she said. "Cyanide."

He drew in a sharp breath. "Did he tell you what was in them?"

"No," said Lois, "I took some from a bottle he kept in a cupboard. He always had them by him. I've heard him say that he would rather die than be caught. I felt the same, so I took them."

"How did you know what was in them?" Roger asked.

"He once told Malone in my hearing."

Roger wished he could understand why she had for so long been determined to keep silent. She must have realized the gravity of the situation. Time and time again she had been compelled to face up to it, and yet until almost the last she had refused to speak. Then, for the first time, he wondered whether she had told *all* the truth. He was going to assure Chatworth that she had, meant to use his influence to make sure that she was not victimized. But could there be something else?

He was uneasy when he walked up the steps of the Yard and yet he did and said nothing to give Lois an inkling of his doubts. Although it was late, he took her to Abbott's office. He wished some other Superintendent were in charge. Surprisingly, however, Abbott greeted her without a fuss, listened to the story, and then spoke reassuringly. Perhaps Abbott understood something of the nervous strain on the girl, and the importance of what might come from it. At all events, the man did nothing to make Lois regret her decision. Less than an hour afterwards, Roger took her across the dark square and through the gates to Cannon Row, where she was housed in one of the rooms, not a cell. Roger saw her smile, and could not believe that she had deceived him, yet he still remained uneasy.

Only when he was back in Abbott's office did he realize that his anxiety about Malone's possible actions had, for once, been unjustified.

Then he told Abbott about Mortimer Oliphant.

20

Janet Delivers News of Importance

"What do you suggest we do, West?" asked Abbott.

"I don't think we should act too quickly, do you?" Roger said. Abbott shook his head. "We've this list of names to investigate and when we've interviewed each man we should have a better idea of what it's all about."

Abbott looked surprised.

"The disposal of stolen goods, surely?"

"Only that?" asked Roger.

"Do you think there's something else?"

"They've gone pretty far for simple fencing," Roger pointed out. "I think we ought to keep an open mind." He shrugged his shoulders. "Theorizing isn't going to help much, but Pickerell wouldn't keep tablets of cyanide of potassium handy because he was afraid of being picked up for trafficking in looted goods."

"No," admitted Abbott, "I had missed the significance of that."

"And I think it rules out the more straightforward crimes," Roger went on. "It could be espionage very carefully hidden."

"You've no hard and fast ideas?"

"I wish I had. All I feel is that it's something of exceptional size. Malone's gang, Oliphant, the Society—suggesting something which had been working for nearly three years—the murder of Joe Leech and, probably, that of Mrs. Cox, all these things together prove a formidable business, which no ordinary motive will account for."

Abbott pressed the tips of his thin fingers together, admitting:

"I am inclined to agree."

"And, of course, the Society is of primary importance," Roger said. "I wish I were more sure of Mrs. Cartier. Perhaps she got in touch with me for some ulterior motive of her own and hasn't told me all the truth. Have you had reports on her and her husband?"

"Yes," said Abbott. He pushed a file across. "Read the reports—there's no hurry."

The office, on the third floor of the Yard, was very quiet as Roger read through the report of Mrs. Cartier. She was of French birth but had become a naturalized Englishwoman in 1946—the year before her marriage to Sylvester Cartier. Daughter of a wealthy Lyons merchant, she had been educated in England for several years. She had been one of the first to offer hospitality to refugees from the iron curtain countries. According to the report, she had first thought of the League of European Relief when she had been approached by some East Germans of the professional classes. There were many cases of hardship. She had helped them and then extended her activities. The Society had been in being for a little more than a year and had a great deal in its favor. Wealthy Europeans in England and on the Continent had contributed towards the funds. Apparently Mrs. Cartier herself did most of the canvassing for money. There was nothing surprising in the fact that she obtained good results; most men would have found the way from their hearts to their pockets after a visit from Mrs. Sylvester Cartier!

There was nothing beyond that and the fact that she had married Sylvester Cartier in 1947.

The second report, on her husband, was much more brief. Cartier had inherited a large fortune from his father, and Roger suddenly realized why the name was so familiar. *Cartier's Food Products*, of course! They were known everywhere; the name was almost as familiar as Heinz, Chef or Brand. He felt annoyed with himself for having missed it.

Educated at Eton and Balliol, a dilettante, a collector of *objets d'art* and antique furniture, Cartier appeared to have lived a life of leisured ease. He was on the directors' board of *Cartier's Food Products* but apparently took little active interest in the company's affairs. He had been prominent in polo circles, had travelled widely, had a much-renowned library, dabbled in philately, was a member of three exclusive clubs. "Correct" was the word to apply to Sylvester Cartier; no man's record could have been more in keeping with his elegant appearance. He always wintered in France. He had a house at Weybridge—Roger remembered seeing that in the telephone directory—as well as a flat in London under his wife's name, and a large country house in Dorset.

Roger finished and looked up.

"There isn't much to glean from those, is there?"

"Not a great deal about either of them," said Abbott. "What the report doesn't say is that Cartier has always mildly disapproved of his wife's activities."

Roger shrugged. "He would probably think that helping refugees was for the common people. Who are the family solicitors?"

Abbott smiled bleakly. "Not Oliphant! Rogerson, Keene, Keene and Rogerson, of Grays Inn Fields. Quite irreproachable."

"Yes, I know." Roger stood up and began to pace the office. "They're both so irreproachable that it seems almost too good to be true and yet I can't help feeling that I am spreading suspicions too widely. Mrs. Cartier might have meant everything she said. If Malone had the slightest suspicion that she was one of his employers, he wouldn't have treated her so roughly. We'd better concentrate on the list of names and addresses."

"Yes," said Abbott. "Especially Oliphant."

"Will you leave him to me?" Roger asked.

"To you?" asked Abbott, slowly, and then more briskly. "Yes, perhaps that's wise, West. You won't encourage Lessing or this friend of Miss Randall's to do too much of their own accord, will you?"

Roger smiled. "They'll be good, I assure you!"

Two taxis passed him but were occupied. It would not take him twenty minutes to walk to the Legge Hotel, yet the fact that he could not get a cab annoyed him, and he thought longingly of his car. There was a garage at the hotel; it might be a good idea to go to Chelsea and drive to Buckingham Palace Gate.

Where was that taxi-driver, Dixon?

Roger had telephoned the house several times, but Morgan's man had nothing to report. He had asked Cornish, earlier in the day, to try to trace the man; no news meant that Cornish had failed. Dixon had followed Cartier's Daimler; the fact that he had not returned was peculiar.

He reached the hotel and told the others what had happened but was still preoccupied. There was no answer when he called Bell Street, but just before he went to bed the telephone rang. It was an apologetic Cornish who hoped he hadn't brought Roger out of bed.

"Oh, no," said Roger. "Have you found that cabby for me?"

"You mean Dixon?" said Cornish. "No, I haven't, Roger. In fact, I meant to tell you earlier in the day that I was put on to another job and couldn't follow it up myself. I did find out that he worked from a small Peckham garage, and I've just had a word with the night duty foreman. He says that Dixon hasn't been home since yesterday morning. His wife had called only a few minutes before I did."

"That's odd," Roger said.

"Yes," Cornish dropped that subject and went on: "I've been with Smith of AZ Division most of the day, trying to find Malone and Pickerell. We haven't had any luck. Malone's reputation is worse than I thought it was. I should keep my eyes open, if I were you."

"I've just about sized him up," Roger said.

"I hoped you would. How are things in general?"

"I suppose I shouldn't grumble," Roger said.

Cornish rang off and Roger returned to the lounge. He stood in front of the fireplace with his hands deep in his trousers pockets. Mark contemplated him with a frown of concentration. Janet had gone to bed and Tennant was pretending to be immersed in an evening paper.

Roger looked at him.

"Do you feel tired?" he asked.

"Who, me?" Tennant dropped the paper and jumped up. "I'm never tired."

"Who, me?" asked Mark, forlornly.

"Both of you," said Roger. "I think we'd better keep an eye on Oliphant's house. Do you know where it is, Mark?"

"He's in Cheyne Walk, just round the corner from a flat I used to have," said Mark. "Any instructions?"

"Just keep a lonely vigil," Roger said with a grin.

The others seemed glad of the opportunity to go out, but when they had gone Roger began to wonder whether it were wise. Abbott had been generous when he had asked to be allowed to handle Oliphant, but it might have been better to have put Yard men to watch him. The danger was that Oliphant would probably recognize a Yard man at sight.

Roger went to bed; Janet, now that Lois had gone, was less on edge and she looked very tired and spoke sleepily from the pillows.

"Back home tomorrow," she said. "We needn't stay here now, darling, need we?"

"No reason at all," Roger assured her.

An Irish maid brought morning tea at eight o'clock. The sun shone through the net curtains at the window and made even the grey slate roofs of adjoining buildings look bright and cheerful. Downstairs, the BBC announcer reading the news had bright things to say about the economic state of the nation.

Janet was fresh-eyed as she sat up in bed, but when she got up she felt dizzy and sat down again abruptly. Startled, Roger said:

"Are you all right?"

"Er—yes, I'm fine," said Janet. She was smiling, although she looked pale, the change in her since she had got out of bed was astonishing. "Darling," she said in an unsteady voice, "sometimes you're as blind as a bat!"

"Oh," said Roger. "Am I?"

"I've suspected it for some time but I wanted to be really sure. I *was* sure on my birthday, but I couldn't worry you after Abbott came."

"What *are* you talking about?" demanded Roger, completely mystified.

Janet's eyes were dewy. "Darling," she said, "doesn't morning sickness mean anything to you?"

"Morning—" Roger began, and then his expression altered, he stared incredulously, started to speak but became tongue-tied. He moved and looked down at her as she stared at him, smiling. He gasped: "No! No, darling, not a baby!"

"Well," said Janet. "It's five years since we were married, or had you forgotten? The marvel is that it didn't happen before." She laughed. "What shall we call him, if it's a boy?"

Roger felt like a man in a dream.

He should have realized it for several days past, or at least suspected it. Everything which had puzzled him was explained, her excitability and quick changes of mood, the ease of her tears, her occasional moments of acerbity.

His first reaction was of delight tinged with anxieties about the little luxuries that he would not be able to provide because of the war. A more urgent matter was the possibility that in his amazement he had made her think that he was lukewarm about it. *Had* he been sufficiently enthusiastic? Or had he depressed her?

He had left her to do the packing while he went on to open the house, to get the car and to get in touch with Mark before going to the Yard. He had only vaguely outlined his own program and he hardly gave a thought to Malone and Oliphant. His mind could not grapple with those problems as well as digest Janet's news. He traveled by taxi and now and again caught himself grinning inanely; when he did so he closed his mouth firmly. Once, when he lit a cigarette, he began to grin so widely that it dropped from his lips. He smothered an exclamation of annoyance, then surrendered himself for five minutes to an orgy of self-congratulation.

It would be easier to make a detour and drive along the Embankment where he expected to find either Tennant or Mark. He saw young Tennant, and wondered what had possessed him to give a job which required an expert to Lois's fiancé, and was relieved that Mark must be somewhere in the offing.

Tennant started.

"Oh, it's you, is it?" said the tousled young man. "I thought it was another copper. I've been asked what I'm doing here twice already."

Roger smiled and Tennant went on:

"What are *you* so pleased about?"

"Oh, I'm not pleased," said Roger. "Where's Mark?"

"At the other end of the street."

"Has anything happened?"

"No one's gone in or out of the place."

"They will," said Roger. "It's a tiresome business, but don't get impatient. This is what you worried me to give you, after all!"

"I didn't think a policeman's job was so dull!"

"Tell Mark I'll have you relieved at half past ten, will you? And then perhaps you'll come to my place and sleep there?"

"If it's all right with you, it wouldn't be a bad idea," said Tennant.

Roger returned to his taxi and his good spirits gained the ascendancy. Nothing could go wrong on such a morning.

He paid off the cabby outside his house and hurried along the path, whistling. He opened the front door, stepped through and closed it, then frowned, because the house was in darkness. He groped for the hall switch and pressed it down; still there was no light.

"The bulb's gone!" said Roger. He went forward a step and put his hand inside the lounge door, pressing that switch down. This time the light made him narrow his eyes, and blinded him with its flare. Then his features stiffened and he stared about him in growing stupefaction.

Nothing was in order.

Against the wall, the piano was in pieces, gaping open, every string broken and hanging loose. The carpet had been slashed across and across, and left in little strips. An armchair had not only been ripped open but the wooden framework had been chopped to pieces. Everything breakable was broken, everything tearable was torn, pictures were down, the wallpaper was covered with great daubs of red paint. It was a scene of such devastation that at first he did not realize its significance.

Then Malone spoke from behind him.

"How do you like it, copper? And what do you know?"

21

Tennant Loses His Temper

Roger stared round at the man.

Malone wore a suit of a blue that was bordering on heliotrope. His marcel waves were dressed with great precision and the grease from his hair made his forehead glisten. He stood with his hands in his pockets and the winged shoulders of his coat were so wide that they nearly touched the door posts on either side. His thin red lips were set in a sneer which he doubtless considered intimidating.

Roger saw all that vaguely.

Far more vivid in his mind's eye was Janet: a composite picture of her gaiety that morning, her joy, the happiness with which she looked forward to coming home, and an imaginary picture of her when she saw the chaos in the lounge. He wondered whether the other rooms had been wrecked; Malone had probably made a thorough job of it.

"Keeping your mouth shut won't help you," said Malone.

A wave of cold anger passed through Roger, visible in his expression. The sneer faded from Malone's face and was replaced by a wary look.

"Listen—" he began.

Roger said: "Malone, I charge you with causing wilful bodily harm to a number of persons, with conspiring to defraud, with theft and looting. I arrest you in the name of the law and warn you that anything you say may be used in evidence. Do you hear me?"

Malone said: "You're crazy!"

"You're under arrest," Roger said. "Anything you do now will be an attempt to resist arrest. I don't know whether we can get you for murder, but even if we can't, be very careful. Next to murder, violence to a policeman will be the most serious charge on the calendar."

"You're off your nut," Malone said, still very wary. "You can't do a thing, West."

"You poor fool!" said Roger, scathingly. "You really think you can get away with it? Every policeman in this country is after you. You haven't even a hope of keeping away from them for the rest of the day. Whatever you do will only make it worse for yourself. If you give yourself up and make a statement, you might get a lighter sentence. It's your only real hope."

"Shut your trap!" snapped Malone, "I didn't come here to listen to talk from you."

"I'm not interested in why you came," said Roger. "I've told you the truth and if you like to play the fool, that's up to you. I don't know how many men you've got with you—"

"I brought plenty," Malone said, his eyes narrowed. "Quit the spieling, West. No one can touch me. How much do you know?"

"As much as everyone at the Yard knows," Roger said. "We'll be moving later in the day."

Malone said thinly: "West, I reckon your wife will be coming here soon. Once before, I took her away to warn you what would happen if you stuck your head out too far. Now it's coming. If you don't talk, I'll deal with her different." He kept his hands in his pockets, where Roger suspected that he had a knife, perhaps a gun. Mention of Janet brought a revival of the cold fury; it made him tremble from head to foot and he had to fight against throwing himself at the gangster—the one fatal thing to do. "You saw me deal with that Cartier dame," Malone continued, "that was nothing to what I'll do to your wife. Tell me what you know."

“Why Cox killed his wife,” said Roger.

Malone moved.

His trick of ending immobility in a sudden cyclonic movement succeeded in taking Roger by surprise. He backed away but caught his foot against a part of the broken chair and staggered against the mantelpiece. Malone struck him with the flat of his hand. It did not account for the sharp, stinging pain in Roger’s cheek nor the warm trickle of blood. He saw the man’s hand in front of him, a razor blade held between the middle and index fingers. He knew that Malone would gladly batter him as he had the room; yet he was less afraid than angry.

“That’s just a little idea of what’s coming to you,” Malone said thinly. “Did the Randall dame talk?”

“She didn’t need to.”

“That’s a lie. Did she talk?”

Roger said: “I’ve warned you, Malone.”

Malone sneered. “I’ve heard busies before. Talk, that’s about all they can do. If you caught me you couldn’t keep me.” He raised his hand threateningly. By a sleight of hand he moved the blade so that it was held between the tips of his fingers. He made a sweeping movement and the blade passed within an inch of Roger’s eyes. For the first time Roger felt only fear of what could have happened.

“I’ll give you two minutes,” Malone said.

From outside there came a shrill whistle, similar to the one that Roger had heard at Mrs. Cartier’s flat and that Mark had heard in the “Saucy Sue.” Malone stiffened and half turned his head. Roger kicked at him, aiming for his groin. He caught the man’s thigh and Malone lost his balance, just as two of the gang came into the room.

They ignored him as Malone, recovering his balance, said: “Who is it?”

“Lessing,” a rat-faced man said. “And the yob with the curly hair.”

Malone’s eyes narrowed. “Tennant, huh? I’ve been wanting to talk to him. How far away?”

"The end of the street."

"Walking?"

"Yeah."

Roger wondered: "Why have they come so soon?"

Malone did not look at Roger, but one of his companions stayed close. He had a knuckle-duster in his hand, an ugly, spiked weapon which would tear a man's face to pieces.

"Don't even squeak," Malone flung at Roger, savagely.

Footsteps sounded on the pavement and then the gravel drive. There was a pause and a heavy knock at the front door. Malone did not move except to put out a hand towards the light switch as if he were going to plunge the room in darkness. If he did—

The man with the knuckle-duster moved swiftly, caught Roger's right wrist, and twisted his arm behind his back. Whoever was outside knocked again; then Mark called:

"Anyone at home?" There was a pause before a key scraped in the lock; Mark had a key to the house.

Malone flicked his finger; the light went out.

"What the—" began Mark, as if startled by the darkness. Actually it was broken by light streaming in from the open front door. "Roger!" Mark called. "Are you in?"

The pressure at Roger's wrist increased and he felt the scraping of the knuckle-duster on his cheek. The veins swelled up in his neck and on his forehead, his breathing was heavy. He knew exactly what would happen if he called out. Damn it, he must call! He opened his lips.

Malone switched on the light. Mark gasped. Roger saw two men standing in the hall and guessed that one of them was showing a gun. Malone stepped into the hall with the sliding, swaggering gait which characterised him.

"Come right in, Lessing," he said. "You're very welcome." He grinned. "Where's Tennant?"

"*Here's* Tennant!" a man called. It was Tennant himself. There was a flurry of movement, a gasp and a shadow which loomed in the hall. It happened so suddenly that Roger felt his captor relax. He took the opportunity and wrenched his wrist away, back-heeled and caught the man's shin. Two men crashed down in the hall, carried to the floor by Bill Tennant, who had leapt past Mark and sailed through the air. He landed on his feet, crouching, and looked at Malone and the other man. Malone held a knife now. There was a split second of silence, a hush while the two men weighed each other up. Malone was crouching and Tennant standing upright with his hands a little way in front of him. The men on the floor began to move.

Roger took a step forward.

Tennant jumped, feet foremost. His heels landed on Malone's stomach, and Malone's hand, holding the knife, swept round aimlessly. There was a squelching sound as Tennant's feet sank into him and he fell backwards, cracking his head against the floor. The man whom Roger had kicked drew back his fist with the knuckle-duster ready, but Tennant came on, keeping his balance by some miracle. He gripped the wrist which held the knuckle-duster, and Malone's man gasped and was thrown against the wall with a thud which shook the house. Malone, scrambling to his feet and with no fight left in him, shouted for help, but no one came.

Tennant turned on him and laughed into his face.

"This is what you hand out, Malone," he said. He struck the man with great power and Malone toppled backwards. "That," Tennant said, "is for Lois. That is for Mrs. Cartier." He bent down and yanked Malone to his feet.

There were men's voices, heavy footsteps and the sound of scuffing in the kitchen. Roger wondered who else had come. Mark was standing just in sight, with a gun in his hand; the two men whom Tennant had first attacked were backing towards the stairs. A familiar voice called:

"Is West all right, Lessing?" It was Cornish!

"Yes," Mark called.

"*Mister* Malone," said Tennant, softly, "I never did like you." The gangster was helpless, hardly able to stand on his feet, but Tennant lifted him by the waist and flung him against the wall.

Then Cornish and two or three plainclothes men came in with

a rush. Tennant drew back. Roger could not look at Cornish, only at Tennant, to see the way he relaxed, the sudden fading of the glitter in his eyes, and the half-ashamed smile which curved his lips.

"It looks as if I lost my temper," he said.

"Temper!" gasped Cornish.

Roger drew a deep breath. "What brought you?" he demanded.

Mark sauntered into the room, looking pleased with himself.

"Malone sent one of his men to see Oliphant," he said. "I recognized him from the "Saucy Sue," and we had a little talk with him on the Embankment. Tennant didn't take long to make him open his mouth! He said Malone was waiting here for you or Janet so I phoned the Yard."

"You see, it was simple," said Tennant. He looked into Malone's face. "I hope I haven't killed him," he said. "I've been giving unarmed combat lessons for two years and as I haven't fought in earnest yet, I thought Malone would do for some real practice!" He put his hands into his pockets and then, for the first time, seemed to notice the chaos of the room. "By George!" he exclaimed. "What a mess!" His eyes widened and he stared at Roger. "What have you done to your face?"

Roger fingered his slashed cheek, surprised to find blood on his fingers.

"I'd better wash this off," he said, and went to the bathroom. As he dabbed at his cheek, which kept bleeding, and while Mark began to dress the cut, things began to take on a proper perspective. "Simple" was the operative word. He remembered seeing the vaguely familiar man near the Embankment and remembered that he had been at the Cartiers' flat, but for once Mark had had the better memory for faces. By sending Mark and Tennant to Oliphant he had done the right thing, after all. No one at the Yard would have recognized the messenger.

"Feeling better?" Mark asked, when sticking plaster was in position.

"I'm all right," Roger said. "So we've got Malone."

"*And* most of his men," Mark said. "But—what utter swine! I—what's the matter? Roger, what—"

"The other rooms!" snapped Roger.

Two minutes later, he had been in every room in the house and felt better, for only the lounge had been touched. He even found himself wondering whether it would be possible to make Janet come in the back way so that she would not get the full force of the shock that the lounge would be bound to give her. He looked at Mark, and explained what had suddenly preoccupied him; at that moment a Black Maria drew up outside. There was a crowd of people waiting and staring, a few dogs at the heels of the crowd, some schoolboys and two or three uniformed men. Masher Malone's party was taken to the van, handcuffed together in twos. Malone, only just able to stagger, went last. Two plainclothes men climbed in, the driver started the engine and the van moved off.

"Any more for any more?" boomed Tennant.

"You've had enough for one day," Mark assured him. "Don't ever take a dislike to me, will you?"

"That depends," grinned Tennant. "Well, what *are* you going to do next, Roger?"

"Who did you leave to watch Oliphant?" Roger demanded.

"Now come off it," said Mark. "We had our work cut out to rescue you from a dreadful fate, we had to take a chance somewhere. Shall we go back there?"

Roger said: "No." He looked at the silent, rather subdued Cornish and there was a faint smile on his face. Cornish probably felt grieved because he had missed the fight. "It's time I remembered I'm a policeman and worked by regulation."

"You mean, interview Oliphant yourself?" Mark asked.

"Yes. I'd better have a word with Abbott first," said Roger. "Mark, will you stay up until Janet arrives?"

"Of course."

"Thanks," said Roger. "I think I'll get the car out," he went on. "You'd better stay around for a bit, Corny."

"Very well," said Cornish.

Roger went out by the back door. The police had forced a window but Cornish had entered using the back door key which had been replaced in the tool-shed by Morgan's man. There were signs of the struggle when the police had first entered but the kitchen looked in perfect order compared with the lounge. Roger scowled as he took out his keys, yet realized he had a great deal to be thankful for; when he thought of Malone he touched his cheek.

A single slip had finished Malone. It was difficult to believe that the man was on his way to the police-cells, that the striking arm of the Pickerell-Oliphant organization had been paralyzed. The sooner he interviewed Malone the better; not that he expected the man to squeal, although probably some of his gang would. Roger forgot his anxieties and the disappointment awaiting Janet in a sudden burst of confidence. If anything puzzled him at the moment he opened the doors of the garage, it was that Tennant had behaved in a peculiar way, to say the least.

The garage doors were wide open when he looked inside. His car was there, bonnet towards him. Sitting at the wheel, eyes wide open and mouth hidden by a scarf tied very tightly, sat a man with a peaked cap pushed to the back of his head, and his hands tied to the steering wheel.

22

Interview with Chatworth

It was Dixon, the missing taxi-driver.

He could not speak even when Roger removed the scarf, and his mouth would hardly close; great red ridges showed on either side. His hands were so stiff that Roger had to prise them from the steering wheel. He had called for help, and Mark and Cornish, Tennant and two other policemen appeared outside the garage.

Roger helped the man from the car. They carried him into the house, put him on a settee, then began to massage his lips and legs and wrist. Mark laced strong tea with brandy and spoon-fed the man. The tension, which had relaxed after the disappearance of the Black Maria, was more acute than ever. Roger was desperately anxious to find out what had happened to Dixon, and who had brought him here.

It was half an hour before the man could speak, and then only in a voice a little above a whisper.

Dixon had followed the Daimler to Bonnock House. Soon after he had parked his cab at the end of the road, another had arrived, bearing Mrs. Sylvester Cartier. With her had been a man whom the taxi-driver knew by sight because he had worked a great deal in the East End and had often been to the Old Bailey for a free entertainment. The man's name, he said, was Oliphant.

"Oliphant!" Roger exclaimed.

"Sure—and the lady." Dixon moistened his lips. "Maybe I got too curious, mister. I went too close. I was hanging around and Malone arrived—you know Malone? He's poison, he—"

"He's at Cannon Row," Roger said.

Dixon's eyes glittered. "I wish I could have had a go at 'im first. Well, I just stayed around. Malone was watching. The toff who had been with the lady came out and got into the Daimler again and I started to follow but before I got far Malone came on the running board. Know Hampstead Heath, mister? Well, it's lonely enough, an' I couldn't do a thing about it. There was four of them." His voice grew hoarse with anger. "They tied me up an' put me at the back of me own cab an' drove it 'ere!"

Roger said: "Have you been here ever since?"

"Every ruddy minnit," said Dixon. "They never even give me a drink o' water. They tied me 'ere an' told me I'd be lucky if anyone came before I was stiff." He gulped. "I couldn't move me 'ead, Guv'nor."

"Did they talk much?"

"Talk—they never did nothing else!" said Dixon. "They arst me 'ow long I'd been a squealer, me—me, a perishing nose! They wanted to know if I'd been told to watch the lady, an' whether you had said anything about her. I said you said I was to watch the toff, Guv'nor. I didn't see no sense in giving them what they perishin' well wanted."

"Good man," applauded Roger.

"That tickled Malone," Dixon said. "He laughed as if it was the best joke in the world, Guv'nor—but *I* had the laugh on him, because he didn't know you was really after the dame."

"And is that the lot?" asked Roger.

"Seems plenty to me," said Dixon. "If I don't get some shut-eye soon I shall drop dead, that's what I shall do."

"We'll get you home," Roger said.

"Guv'nor, if you've got a bed here, I'll be asleep in a couple of jiffs."

"Yes, of course." Roger left Mark and Tennant to put the man to bed, smiled at the thought of Janet's homecoming, then drove in his own car to the Yard. There seemed nothing to do but detain Mrs. Cartier and Oliphant and hope that one or the other would make a true statement. The woman might break down. Some things continued to puzzle him. If Malone had known that the woman was implicated when Dixon had arrived, he must have known later that evening, yet there had been nothing phoney about the way he had assaulted her.

"To make me jump to the wrong conclusion," Roger mused. "It couldn't mean anything else."

He reached the Yard and immediately gave instructions for Mrs. Cartier and Oliphant to be shadowed. He learned from Eddie Day that Abbott had put a man on Oliphant after all; so Abbott was still capable of being two-faced. Until he saw Abbott, he thought that Mrs. Cartier had no watcher, but he was wrong. The Superintendent was apologetic; Chatworth had ordered him to have Oliphant watched, as well as Mrs. Cartier; the AC had not been prepared to leave it to Roger. And:

"I think he was right, West."

"So do I, by hindsight," admitted Roger. "Any sign of Pickerell?"

"No."

"Have you heard about Malone?"

"I've just come from him," said Abbott. "He will not talk, but then, he is hardly in a condition to, he will be in hospital for several days. Who dealt with him? Was it Cornish?"

Roger smiled. "No. There was a bit of a scrap. I can't say who hit who."

He expected to be pressed on the point, but a buzzer rang on Abbott's desk and the Superintendent stood up quickly.

"That will be Sir Guy. I told him you had arrived and he promised to ring for us as soon as he was ready." Abbott led the way up to Chatworth's office and they went in immediately.

"You're having quite a week, aren't you, West?" The question was almost aggressive.

Roger grimaced. "Yes, aren't I?"

"It looks as if the worst is over," observed Chatworth.

"Abbott's told you that we're watching everyone?" Roger nodded. "All the people whom the Randall girl named have been interviewed except Oliphant," Chatworth went on. "We've been very busy all through the night."

Roger smiled with relief. He should have realized that the Yard would act swiftly and thoroughly. He had not yet got it out of his system that he was working this case on his own.

"And we have a very remarkable story," Chatworth said. "You haven't told him, Abbott, have you?"

"No, sir."

Roger stared. "What is it, sir?" he asked.

"It is a combination of things. First, many of the stolen jewels have not been disposed of. Pickerell sold others to some of the people to whom Miss Randall took the packages—she actually carried the stolen goods. The proceeds of many jewel thefts, here and on the Continent, passed through the hands of Pickerell and Lois Randall. Pickerell was the fence, always working from Welbeck Street."

"Yes?" said Roger. Chatworth's manner told him there was more to come.

Chatworth gave an almost smug smile.

"And then there was the *real* purpose of the Society of European Relief, West! Relief!" He threw back his head and uttered a short laugh. "Oh, it had its genuine side, but the chief angle was *very* clever indeed. Jewels were brought in from the Continent, sometimes by refugees, who owned them, others by thieves posing as refugees, and more—the largest proportion—jewels hidden away during the last war, and discovered. There's been a lot of smuggling, we've known that for some time. Jewels flooded the Society from all sources and they were all handled at Welbeck Street."

Roger thought: "Smuggled sparklers, so that's it." He felt annoyed with himself for being disappointed.

"Most of them came from Germany and Italy," Chatworth said, gently.

Roger stared: "*Ger*many?"

"You've heard of the fortunes which Goering, Goebbels, Himmler and the rest of them are supposed to have wafted away?" asked Chatworth. "Of course you have! But other well-placed Nazi officials and German business men weren't able to do it. They wanted to save something from the wreckage, so they put their money in jewels—many of them pillaged from the occupied countries—and they sent them over here. The Society of European Relief became an organization"—Chatworth laboured over the words—"which relieved a great many people of their jewels, took jewels from others for services never fully rendered, and became a gigantic world-wide sales organization. Some of its members, posing as refugees, travelled abroad and sold stolen jewels. Follow that, West? The Society of European Relief did all these things."

Roger said gruffly: "So it was as big as that."

"Oh, yes," said Chatworth. "And think how clever it was. They actually had a genuine organization ready for distributing the jewels, which were never allowed to remain in one country for long. For every genuine applicant for relief there was one who was a party to this scheme. There were people with friends behind the Iron Curtain prepared to help when Mrs. Cartier persuaded them—men who wouldn't profit from the jewels themselves, but were prepared to hold them. I don't know what precious argument the woman puts up. She probably told a lot of them that they were jewels belonging to refugees from Russia, Poland, all of Eastern Europe. There are some very big names on the list of patrons of the Society—oh, it will prove quite a scandal! Beginning to understand how important it was that you should not have been allowed to connect the murder of the woman Cox with this?"

Roger said: "I certainly do. But it's doubtful whether I ever would have done."

"Oh, I don't know," said Chatworth. "I think Oliphant must have been afraid that you had seen or noticed something of significance. I've heard from some of the people concerned that they have been afraid of a raid for several months. They had the wind-up all right and"—he laughed—"Friday the 13th worried someone!"

Roger said: "Ye-es. It couldn't have been that alone. You've enough on Mrs. Cartier and Oliphant to arrest them, I suppose?"

"We can pick them up whenever we want to," said Chatworth. "It is now established that Oliphant has been to see Malone on several occasions. Also, he was at Cox's house with Malone just before you arrived on December 13th."

Roger caught his breath.

"They assumed you'd seen or heard them together, and one day you were bound to realise the significance," Chatworth went on. "Well, I've left Oliphant and Mrs. Cartier to you! It's your job to charge them."

Roger sat back in his chair and said after a pause:

"Thank you, sir. I wonder if we would be wise to defer arresting Mrs. Cartier."

"Now, West!"

"I see it this way," said Roger. "She came to see me and first awoke my interest in the Society. If she hadn't pretended that she wanted my wife's help, I would probably never have gone to Welbeck Street. We might have traced Malone to Bonnock House, but even that's doubtful. After a long time we might have realized that the Society was a cover for crime, though I'm not sure. But for Mrs. Cartier we wouldn't have been able to make a move and I would still be under suspension."

"Come, West, come! Grow up!" Chatworth's sarcasm was heavy as a spade. "She has been a very smart—clever woman, no doubt about that." He looked over the tops of his glasses. "Why, she even got five guineas out of me for her precious Society!" He hurried over that evil memory and went on, scowling: "She told you some things and she meant to be sure that whatever else, you would not suspect her."

Roger said: "I don't know about that. I saw Malone strike her. I saw the way her head went from side to side. That wasn't faked—he hurt her. I can't be wholly sure that she has told me everything," he admitted, "but I can't believe that she would have been fool enough to have given me quite such a direct lead if she were guilty. Then there are the tapes. If you're asking me to believe that Malone went there to get one just to create effect and to distract attention from her—well, sir, I can't believe it."

"Oh," said Chatworth. "Well, what *do* you think?"

"If she did lead me there and is a party to the crimes it would only be because the Society is no longer useful and that she has taken up the second line of defense or else the people who work with her did. On the other hand, if she were genuinely interested in the Society as a relief organization and had reason to believe that it was being used for something else, she acted rationally."

"I see your point," Chatworth said.

"So do I," agreed Abbott.

"I'm simply trying to imagine whether anyone else could be behind it," Roger said. "If we have the list of the supporters of the Society we've plenty to choose from. We may only be at the fringe of the affair yet. Seriously, sir—I ask you to pull Oliphant in if you must, but leave Mrs. Cartier."

Chatworth said after a long pause:

"I'll think about it. Have a couple of men ready to go with you to Chelsea, for Oliphant, in case we act at once. I'll call you in a few minutes."

"Very good, sir," said Roger, formally.

He wished he could hear what Abbott said to the AC as he went to his own office. This was empty, and he was glad that he could sit back at his desk without being harassed by curious officers. He hated the thought that had come to him, he wished that it had not.

Supposing a man at the Yard *was* taking bribes?

Supposing the whole thing had been built up so that suspicion, which would be inevitable, had fallen on him, not on the real culprit.

Abbott?

Malone had said the Yard couldn't keep him if they got him. Was his confidence founded on the fact that he was sure of help from inside the Yard?

The telephone rang and he answered it quickly, surprised to hear Chatworth so soon on the line: he had not yet even detailed the sergeants. Then Eddie Day came in breezily, his prominent teeth bared in a smile of welcome.

"Eddie, get two sergeants here for me, will you? I'll be back soon," Roger said. "I'm going to see the Old Man."

Mention of Chatworth was quite enough to prevent Eddie from trying to delay him. He walked quickly along the corridor and up the stairs, entering on Chatworth's gruff "come in."

Abbott had gone.

"Close the door, West," said Chatworth. "Sit down and tell me what's on your mind."

"I think I've told you ev—" Roger began.

"No you haven't!" Chatworth barked. "Something is worrying you, I saw your change of expression while you were here before. What is it?"

Reluctantly, Roger said: "I still can't understand why I was framed. The Oliphant-Malone coincidence might be enough and yet it doesn't make sense."

"Ah!" said Chatworth. He leaned forward, pressing the backs of his hands against the side of the desk. "Does anything else puzzle you? Or have you allowed yourself to be dazzled by your change of fortunes and forgotten to *think?*"

"Do you mean, the manner of my suspension?" Chatworth simply glared. "You were so sure that I was involved—" his mind kept probing. "You took it for granted that I was, didn't you?"

"We *knew* someone was accepting bribes and shutting his eyes to a lot of things. We thought it was you."

"You mean there's still someone?" Roger asked tensely.

"Yes," said Chatworth, and exhaled with a noise like a collapsing toy balloon.

Before Roger could speak after the silence which followed,

the telephone rang. Chatworth frowned, and lifted it promptly. His frown disappeared in an expression of amazement. He said: "Yes, I'll come." He put the receiver down and got up slowly. "Come with me, West," he said. "Malone nearly escaped from his cell. He got a key from somewhere."

Roger exclaimed: "A key!" The significance of that crashed into his mind. "That proves someone here is trying to help Malone."

"It proves it, yes," said Chatworth.

A sergeant and three policemen at Cannon Row had managed to overpower Malone, after he had unlocked the door of his cell and tried to fight his way out of the police station. Cornish had brought Malone and the others here to Cannon Row, and then gone on to the East End. Afterwards, Malone had been visited by Abbott, and later by both Abbott and Tiny Martin.

23

Dishonor Among Police

Chatworth began to speak in a low voice.

He had long suspected that information was leaking from the Yard. Two or three arrests of men wanted for various crimes—all in the East End—had been prevented because the suspects had been warned and had managed to escape; they were now in hiding. After the first two, in the November of the previous year, he had kept a careful watch, and had given Abbott and Tiny Martin the task of trying to find the leakage. There had been other leakages only slightly less serious. Raids on West End clubs had failed because the proprietors had been warned in advance. Two small fences had been able to get rid of stolen jewels before their premises were searched. As far as Roger and the rest of the Yard knew, these were incidentals, cases which had failed at the last moment—as many did, there was nothing unusual about it. Chatworth had drawn a line between them all.

Abbott had worked quietly. Malone's name had been heard more often and Roger's associated with it. Abbott had tried the obvious thing, and approached Leech.

"And from then on it appeared to be a clear-cut case against you," said Chatworth. "You know what happened after that. The tape-recorder proved that you were not the man. However, there is someone involved. Malone getting the key proves that beyond doubt. You suspect Mr. Abbott, don't you?"

"He's an obvious possibility. He told me that he had seen Malone, and only a policeman could have given Malone the key. But I don't always trust the obvious, sir."

"Charitable of you," growled Chatworth. "Who else?"

"It could be Sergeant Martin, who is familiar with all that Abbott does, and he was at the cell. But it needn't be either of them."

"You think it is but you're trying to be fair," said Chatworth. "All right, West! Mr. Abbott was very anxious that you should arrest Mrs. Cartier immediately, wasn't he? He tried to persuade me to give those instructions, but your case, for her, was a strong one. She must be watched, but there is no need for immediate action. We've uncovered the main plot, we must now find who is letting us down so badly."

"Have you any action in mind, sir?"

"Yes. To use Oliphant as a bait. We won't go for him yet, but will broadcast the fact that it's only a matter of time before we do. I've already given Mr. Abbott those instructions. If Oliphant remains where he is—" the AC shrugged. "It might be that whoever has been selling us out, thinks it will be too dangerous this time. On the other hand, if he tries to get away we can pick him up. In a police force several thousand strong there are bound to be some rogues, but I don't like to think that any of them reach a position of responsibility. There's another thing we have to admit: it has completely disrupted our organization. I've never known so many things go awry at the same time because I haven't felt that I can wholly trust anyone."

Roger had a curious sensation; he actually felt sorry for the AC! Of all the men whom he had imagined able to stand alone Chatworth was the strongest. Now he was confessing that the situation had got beyond him.

Roger smiled. "You know, sir, we aren't doing too badly! Malone and his mob under arrest, the Society racket is uncovered, most of the agents, guilty and innocent, known to us. At another time we'd be congratulating ourselves. Within forty-eight hours we should know whether Mrs. Cartier *is* the brains behind the scheme, or whether it's Oliphant or someone whom we don't yet know."

"Yes," said Chatworth, relaxing into a smile. "Comforting common sense, West. Do you think it possible that whoever is giving information from here *is* the real leader?"

"Vaguely," Roger said. "Are you having any individuals in the force watched?"

"Difficult to set the police to catch the police," Chatworth said, "especially after our one failure. I shall leave it to you."

"With full authority?" Roger asked, quietly.

"With full authority to act. You must tell no one here what you are doing. If you want anyone followed without his knowledge, whoever you use must believe that there is some danger for his quarry and that he's acting as a bodyguard—you can arrange that, of course?"

"Of course, sir," echoed Roger.

Ten minutes later he was sitting at his desk. The office was empty but for himself and he was grinning broadly.

The quick changes of mood which he had felt that day were natural enough.

The telephone rang. "Mrs. West is on the line, sir," the operator told him.

"Put her through," Roger said. "Hallo, Jan! Are you all right?"

"I would like to wring Malone's neck," said Janet. "But I'm told that Bill Tennant didn't do a bad job! Darling, I wanted to tell you not to worry about the lounge. They have left us some furniture, and well, it doesn't really matter all that much. How are things going?"

"Not badly," said Roger, adding appreciatively: "How could it, with a wife like you? Ask Mark and Tennant to meet me at the Green Cat—Mark knows it—at half past two, will you? Unless they're both too tired, that is. I think I can find something for them to do."

"Mark's here," said Janet.

Mark's voice came on the line almost at once. Roger confirmed the arrangement to meet at the Green Cat, and rang off as the door opened and Eddie Day bustled in.

"Now what's the matter with you, Handsome?" demanded Eddie. "Strike me, you look as if you'd lost a tanner and found half a crown! Been promoted?" he added, almost fearfully.

Roger laughed. "No, Eddie, I won't be able to go any higher for years, if at all, so cast the green mote out of your eye!"

Eddie looked positively relieved.

"Things going all right, then?" he asked.

"Not badly at all," said Roger. "You haven't seen Abbott, have you?"

"Just come from him," replied Eddie. "Cold fish all right, he tried to tick me off. Me! *He* doesn't look as if he's come into a fortune, if you ask me he looks as if he's got something on his mind."

"Does he?" asked Roger, innocently.

He made one or two phone calls, wishing Cornish were at the Yard. But the fair-haired Inspector was working in AZ—his old Division—which he knew thoroughly, trying to find out more about Malone and keeping an eye open for Pickerell. Pickerell, Mrs. Cartier and Oliphant, Roger thought, might give him the answer to the major problem, that of the renegade policeman.

"Seen Sloan?" asked Eddie Day, looking up from his desk.

"Sloan? No!" Roger was eager. "Is he back?"

"I saw him coming in, half an hour ago," Eddie said. "Looks as if he's been in a place where the sun shone."

Detective-Inspector William Sloan, until recently Sergeant Sloan and Roger's chief *aide,* was a tall, not bad-looking man, with mousy hair and a rather speculative expression in his brown eyes. Roger sent for him. He said that he had come back early because he had heard a rumor of Roger's trouble.

"Oh, it passed," Roger said, as Eddie Day bustled out. "But the AC feels pretty sure that there is a leakage here." He looked at Sloan steadily. The other did not answer, except with a nod.

"What I want to do," said Roger, "is to make sure that no one makes an attack on either Abbott or Martin." He paused, thinking that Sloan was probably the only man at the Yard, Cornish possibly excepted, who would be able to read between his words. "They've been up to the neck in this business and they might be in danger even though Malone's finished. But then, you don't know what's been happening?"

"I've heard all about it," said Sloan. "I've been in the canteen."

"Good! Take a couple of reliable men, and guard Abbott and Martin with their lives!" Roger smiled. "Don't let Abbott know what you're doing, or he might get annoyed. Phone me if there's anything urgent. Oliphant is Suspect Number 1 at the moment —had you heard of that?"

"Everyone here seems to have heard," Sloan told him.

"Nice work," Roger said.

But he believed that it was a mistake and was glad it was Chatworth's responsibility, not his. If Oliphant were warned, anyone at the Yard might be responsible.

In the next hour, several reports were telephoned to him. The men watching Oliphant had nothing to report. The solicitor had not left his house but had been seen at the front window. He had had no callers. Mrs. Cartier was at her flat, but her husband had gone to the City and had last been seen entering the building which housed the head offices of the Cartier Food Product Company. There was no trace of Pickerell, but Cornish, telephoning personally, said that several more of Malone's men had been located and there were rumors that a man answering Pickerell's description had been seen in the East End the previous evening.

"Good man. Go to it!" Roger said.

"Ought I to have a word with Abbott?" Cornish asked.

"Why not?" asked Roger, putting Cornish through.

He telephoned the letting office at Bonnock House, talked for some time, and at half past twelve, went down to the canteen, had a snack, then left for Pep Morgan's office. He had telephoned to say that he would be there about one o'clock and asked for Pep's chief operatives to be present. Maude greeted him with a cigarette dangling from the corner of her mouth. She told him that she had been to see Pep that morning and that he was making a good recovery.

"That's fine," said Roger. "Where are the men?"

Maude cocked her thumb over her shoulder towards Pep's private office.

Lanky Sam was propping himself up against the window. A stolid, chunky individual—the man who had been at Bell Street and who had left soon after dawn that day—was sitting on Morgan's desk. He swore that he had heard nothing of the taxi-driver's arrival in the garage; Dixon had been put there before Pep's man had arrived on duty. The other men, middle-aged with jaundiced looks in their eyes and the world-weariness which comes to men whose life is bound up with the sordid business of domestic disruption, were sitting on upright chairs. All of them eyed Roger hopefully.

"Okay, Boss," Sam said. "Shoot."

Roger smiled. "I'm no longer the bad boy of the Yard, but I still want some help."

"So you really admit there *are* detectives outside the Yard?" Sam said, admiringly. "You learn quick, Handsome!"

"I hope you will," Roger said. "Listen."

He told them exactly what he wanted.

He thought Sam seemed disappointed but the men went off cheerfully enough.

He telephoned the *Cry* and the *Echo* from Morgan's office, speaking to both Wray and Tamperly. He gave them a *résumé* of the developments and promised them further revelations later in the day. Both men worked for evening as well as daily papers in the same combine, and he said to each:

"If you can get a paragraph in hinting at startling developments in the next twenty-four hours, it would help," he said. "But don't say that I'm cleared."

Each man agreed.

Roger replaced the receiver and saw Maude looking up at him narrowly.

"Have you got something, Handsome?"

"I wouldn't be surprised!" Roger said.

He reached the Green Cat, a small restaurant off Piccadilly, at half past two precisely; he had to wait for ten minutes before Mark and Tennant arrived. At a corner table, where they had coffee, Roger outlined the situation, naming Abbott and Tiny Martin.

"I'm not at all surprised," Mark said.

"Where do we come in, Roger?" asked Tennant.

Roger said: "I'm going to telephone Oliphant and tell him that Mrs. Cartier wants to see him at her flat. Then I shall telephone Mrs. C. and tell her Oliphant is coming, let's say at four o'clock. That will give us time to work."

"Supposing they don't bite?" Mark said.

"Then we'll have to try again."

"Supposing they *do* bite?" demanded Tennant.

Roger smiled. "There's my man! You'll be at hand. There is a flat next to the Cartiers which we can use. The tenants will be out but I've had their permission to use the flat. It has a lounge window next to the Cartiers. Outside Bonnock House there are little balconies and a man of your agility can easily climb from one to the other. I'll be in the Cartiers' lounge and you'll be on the balcony. I'll leave it to you when you come in! They'll probably try to be violent, but that won't worry you! Er—have you ever jumped through a pane of glass?"

Tennant beamed. "I've jumped through everything!" he declared.

"Don't cut yourself," Roger said. "Well now—I'll have to be busy. As soon as the message is phoned to Mrs. Cartier I want her phone disconnected. Then you've got to be installed next door . . ."

He continued, outlining his plans; and by half past three everything was settled. Then he telephoned the Yard, to learn that reports showed no developments except that Sloan had left a message to say that Abbott and Martin had left the Yard, and had gone to AZ Division, that part of the East End which included Rose Street and Leech's pub. Then, before he rang off, he was told that Oliphant had left his Chelsea house at three-fifteen.

Roger was at Piccadilly when he made the inquiries and he drove immediately to Bonnock House. Crossing the Heath, the quickest route, he remembered Dixon's story of its loneliness.

He reached the Cartiers' flat at four-fifteen.

The maid who had reminded him of Pickerell opened the door and told him, a shade too quickly, that neither Mr. nor Mrs. Cartier were at home.

"I'll wait," Roger said.

"I don't think—" the maid began.

Someone in another room said: "No, I don't!"

Roger smiled. "Take my card in, please. Don't make things difficult for yourself."

The maid looked reluctant, but she took the card, approached the door from which the voices were coming and tapped, gingerly. Cartier's voice was sharp.

"What is it?"

"Excuse me, sir, but a gentleman from—"

Roger put his hand to the door and opened it wider. He almost banged into Cartier, who was coming forward. Behind Cartier was his wife, sitting on the settee where she had greeted Roger on that evening which now seemed an age ago. She looked startled but there was hardly any sign left of the rough treatment from Malone.

"What the devil are you doing here?" Cartier demanded.

"I am a police officer," Roger said, formally. "I would like you to answer a few questions, sir."

"Why, West!" exclaimed Mortimer Oliphant, rising from an easy chair and smiling widely. "Well, well, how small a place London is!"

The solicitor's interruption seemed to startle Cartier, who

closed the door on the maid. Mrs. Cartier extended a hand which Roger carefully ignored; that made her frown. Oliphant, well dressed, smiling, handsome in his dark fashion, spoke heartily.

"I'd no idea that you knew West, Mrs. Cartier!"

"Only in the way of business," said Roger. He glanced at the set tea-table, seeing that there was early lettuce, jam, what looked like real cream and cakes and pastries. Mrs. Cartier rang a handbell and the maid appeared.

"Bring another cup for the Inspector," said Mrs. Cartier. "You will have some tea, won't you?"

"Thank you," said Roger, formally.

"We were just discussing a remarkable thing," said Oliphant, who seemed too anxious to talk. "I received a message asking me to visit Mrs. Cartier on Society business and she received one purporting to come from me, but neither of us sent such a message!"

Roger smiled. "No," he said, "I sent them."

Cartier exclaimed: "Mr. West, you may be a policeman, but I insist on an explanation."

"Don't get impatient, darling," urged Mrs. Cartier.

Oliphant said curtly: "That's a surprising admission, West."

"I knew that you and Mrs. Cartier did a great deal of business together and wanted the opportunity of meeting you at the same time. I couldn't think of any other way of arranging it." Roger smiled pleasantly. Oliphant was wary, Mrs. Cartier's smile was obscure, and Cartier appeared to be really bewildered.

Oliphant demanded: "Is this visit official?"

"Haven't I made that clear?" asked Roger.

"In that case—"

"But not necessarily aggressive!" Roger assured him. He settled back in his chair and waited for the maid to bring in another cup and saucer, knife and plate. When she had gone, he went on: "I think I ought to be frank with you, Mrs. Cartier. Your organization had been used to hide the activities of a criminal organization which—"

“But of course!” she interrupted. “I told you it had!”

“I wonder if you realize quite how widespread and powerful an organization it was,” said Roger. “We have been able to find most of the active supporters and many of the people who helped in the work. Unfortunately, we haven’t found who was really directing the organization unless it was someone in this room.”

He beamed.

“You have no right to make such slanderous suggestions!” said Cartier angrily, but he turned to his wife. “From the very beginning I disliked the idea. If you had not interested yourself in such a charity, this would never have happened!”

“Now, darling,” said Mrs. Cartier. “I don’t think—”

“You’re behaving *very* aggressively, West,” accused Oliphant.

“How much did you know about this yourself?” Roger demanded.

For the first time the solicitor looked really worried. “Are you suggesting—”

“Hasn’t your usual informant sent the warning?” asked Roger. “Yes, Oliphant, you, personally. I have a warrant for your arrest. Also I have one for—”

“If you think my wife—” Cartier began, starting violently. He knocked over his cup, which fortunately was empty. The spoon struck a salt-cellar standing near the lettuce, and salt spilled over the table. “Damn!” ejaculated Cartier. He took a pinch of salt and threw it over his left shoulder, talking as he did so. “If you have the impertinence to suggest that my wife was a party to this criminal business, I shall insist—”

He went on and on with Roger eyeing him steadily.

In his mind’s eye he saw Cartier about to follow his wife and stepping into the road to avoid walking under a ladder. He had another picture of Cartier uncrossing dessert knives in this very room. He saw the man throwing salt over his shoulder.

Cartier stopped and Oliphant said: “This is outrageous, West.”

“Is it?” asked Roger grimly. “Mr. Cartier, you are obviously very superstitious. Did my meeting with Oliphant on the 13th of December really upset you so much?"

Cartier stiffened, Oliphant uttered a sharp exclamation, and the room fell very quiet.

24

A Man Brings a Warning

Oliphant broke the silence, making a good show of annoyance and yet pretending not to show it in front of Roger.

"I'm afraid West is getting rather beyond himself," he said. "If he has developed peculiar ideas about unlucky dates, we need hardly treat his visit seriously."

"Oh, but you should," Roger said.

"Damn your impertinence!" snapped Cartier. "I demand a full explanation and an unqualified apology."

Roger shrugged. "You're trying hard, aren't you? Oliphant, we knew last night that you were up to your neck in this, but we waited for you to make a move. You didn't make it so I forced your hand. I expected you to hear from your informant at the Yard, but he's been very remiss, hasn't he?"

"Don't be a fool!" snapped Oliphant.

"I'm not being," Roger insisted. "I've told you that I have a warrant for your arrest. I have one for Mrs. Cartier, too. I can take Cartier away with me, too." He laughed at them all, but the only one who seemed unaffected was the woman. "I thought this little talk would clear the air," he added, cheerfully. "You see, before it's really finished, as far as we are concerned at the Yard we want to find out who has been selling you information and who has been condoning your crimes. Who is it?"

"I have nothing to say, except that this is a grotesque abuse of your authority," Oliphant snapped.

"Who is it, Cartier?" Roger demanded.

"You must be quite mad!" Cartier was almost shrill.

"You wouldn't know, Mrs. Cartier, would you?" asked Roger. When she made no answer he went on: "This isn't working out very well. Everything pointed to Mrs. Cartier but she first gave me reason to suspect the Society, and I couldn't see her deliberately attracting attention to herself. Superstitions played an obvious part, and when I saw a manifestation of superstitiousness on your part, Cartier, I wondered whether your hostility towards the Society was really sincere. I thought if I could get you all here together, with the telephone wires disengaged, and that's easy, for a policeman!—and we had a heart to heart talk, I might be able to put everything in order. If Mrs. Cartier has been an innocent victim of the conspiracy, I don't want to make trouble for her. Mrs. Cartier, you began to suspect what was wrong when you put in the tape-recorder, didn't you? You hoped to find out whether your worst fears were realized. You knew Oliphant was involved, as well as Pickerell and Lois Randall, but you only suspected your husband's complicity."

"West, stop this!" Cartier shouted.

"Be quiet!" snapped Roger, and he was surprised when the man subsided. "Mrs. Cartier, you knew all that was being done. Your husband—as well as you yourself—had friends all over the Continent. You probably started the Society to help those friends who escaped, but I don't think you had any desire to extend the scope of it. It was extended however, and then you became afraid of it. You would not take any direct action until you were sure. You heard that I was being framed, and so you came to see me, hoping that I would add two and two together. Well, here's your answer. Your husband *was* involved."

"There is not a scrap of truth in anything you say," declared Oliphant.

"I'm waiting here for the proof," Roger said. "You've worked through one of the officials at Scotland Yard, that is definitely established. He will make a move, he's bound to because he is afraid that when you are arrested you will betray him. He will come to warn Cartier to get away. He will be told that you, Oliphant, left Chelsea and came here and he'll be equally anxious to warn you. He'll know that in handling the matter I made a significant omission. I didn't have police protection at Bonnock House. He will probably think that I can't handle it on my own."

"Perhaps he does," murmured Oliphant, but Roger ignored him.

"He'll be fairly confident because he has the authority to remove any police who might come to the flats," Roger continued. "That is one of his advantages, isn't it?"

Oliphant said in a queer voice:

"Is it, West?"

"Oh, yes."

"And do you think you know this individual?" asked Oliphant.

"I do," said Roger.

"Perhaps," said Oliphant. "Perhaps you're right, West." He looked at Cartier and said with a twisted smile: "You were certainly right, Sylvester. The 13th undid us."

"Don't be—" began Cartier.

"There's no need to worry," Oliphant said, slowly. "West came alone. He was so anxious to make sure that his colleague didn't become suspicious, and has grandiose ideas about bringing off a coup by himself. He's here alone. We can handle him. If he has a warrant for me, it will be executed, either by him or someone else." There was a curious smile on his face. "West is no fool. He knows that I have been a party to more than one murder—don't you, West? The police have a case for murder against me, as an accessory. There's no hope for me."

"I'm glad you realize it," Roger said.

"But I may as well be hung for a sheep as a lamb," said Oliphant. He put his hand to his pocket and drew out an automatic, levelling it casually at Roger. "If I shoot him," he said dispassionately, "it will put the finishing touches to the case, but you and Antoinette need not suffer. You can tell the whole story—how West thought you were in it, how he accused me, but I confessed to being the leader and how I shot myself after shooting him. It will be quite convincing, won't it?" He looked at Mrs. Cartier, and in spite of his tension, Roger understood why Oliphant should behave like this.

Oliphant was in love with the woman!

"Well, West, what do you think of your scheme now?" Oliphant said.

Roger said slowly: "You told me that *I* wasn't sane."

"Meaning that I'm not? Oh, I don't know," said Oliphant. "I have been feeling the strain lately. Nothing has worked out as I expected, and this will be the most satisfactory end. Don't imagine that I am sacrificing myself for Cartier. I think it is the only way in which—" he drew a deep breath—"*every*one can be happy?"

The woman was looking at him.

"Don't make such admissions!" Cartier cried.

"It can't do any harm," said Oliphant. "Only West is listening and he won't be able to talk, but his men will come before long." He stood up and backed towards the window. "Don't try to stop me, Sylvester. Curious," he added. "I wonder if it would have worked out differently but for your inhibitions? The unlucky 13th—it always frightened you, didn't it? And it seemed so easy to divert suspicion to West, and satisfy you. With West in jail, our real informant would have been quite safe, which was much more important than easing your mind about the 13th! But we don't need to tell West everything, he can fill in the details himself—in the next world!" Oliphant laughed, softly. "When our man comes from the Yard to warn us, he'll find West and me dead. You can tell him what has happened, and he will be able to wind up the case most satisfactorily. You will say that West came here alone to *try to extort more money*. You'll make it plain that he is the renegade after all, the tape was a trick. Then you can start all over again."

He smiled and levelled the gun.

Roger thought: "Hurry, Tennant, hurry!" He fancied that he

had seen a shadow at the window, but was not sure. He wondered whether he had relied too much on "unarmed combat" and the remarkable agility of Bill Tennant. Then he saw the shape at the window, of Tennant standing on the ledge.

Cartier gasped: "Oliphant, look!"

Tennant launched himself against the window, smashing the glass with his elbows and knees, keeping his chin tucked well down; he wore a crash-helmet. The crash made Oliphant swing round, and Roger jumped to his feet and overturned the table. At the same time there was a banging at the door, then footsteps in the hall. Tennant, with a scratch on his right cheek and another on his hand, fell upon Oliphant. They hit the ground together.

The gun flew from Oliphant's hand. Cartier made a movement towards it, but his wife held his wrist.

"No," she said in a tense voice. "No, not that!"

Roger watched this tense drama of human emotions as if he were standing a long way off. It made no difference to the issue, all but one thing was over, now, yet there was a fascination in the relationship between the man and his wife.

Cartier said: "*You* started this, you bitch! If it hadn't been for you this would never have happened."

The door opened and the maid, frightened and trembling, admitted Mark.

Mrs. Cartier said: "I couldn't let it go on, I simply couldn't. But you'll be free one day. Don't do anything to let them hang you. You know nothing about the previous murders."

Cartier struck her savagely across the face. She turned away and Roger put a hand on the man's shoulder.

Tennant was brushing himself down. Oliphant was sitting on the floor, looking up stupidly.

"Well, that didn't take long," Tennant said, almost wistfully. "Anyone else coming, West?"

"Soon, I hope," Roger said.

Neither Oliphant nor Cartier spoke again. Roger handcuffed them to each other in another room, with Mark and Tennant to watch them. He gave the maid careful instructions, then returned to the lounge. Mrs. Cartier was standing by the window, her face expressionless and her cheeks colorless. Roger looked out and saw one of Morgan's men at the street corner, just walking out of sight.

He wondered whether Abbott would come. He did not feel like talking, although he wished the woman would break the silence. Suddenly, she turned and took a cigarette from a box on the table. She looked at him levelly as he lit it for her.

"How long have you known that my husband was involved in the crimes?"

"Not very long," Roger said.

"Did I so much as hint at it?"

"You did not," Roger assured her. "You did all you could, Mrs. Cartier, to hide that. I wish—"

"Please!" she said, then went on slowly. "I have always been afraid of it, but what could I do, what *could* I do? He *is* my husband. I could not bring myself to believe it. Gradually, I learned what was happening, how they worked, what Pickerell did, what poor Lois Randall was forced to do. But for the agonising fear that Sylvester was concerned, I would have told the police much earlier. When I learned about you—" she drew a deep breath. "You know what I did. I told him, also, to warn him. When he did not show any resentment I thought, I prayed, that I was wrong. But that record—the 13th—I knew how superstitious he was, how everything worried him—spilled salt, ladders—a hundred things."

Roger said: "'How much more do you know, Mrs. Cartier?"

"Not much more than you must know already," she said. "Oliphant arranged most of the crimes, I think. My—my husband knew the people whose goods were sent here. He was always friendly with those in authority on the Continent, but so were many others. I knew a little of Malone. I learned much from tapes which you have not heard; I hid them, but you will be able to use them now." She went on tonelessly. "They showed up everything, Inspector. One says that the man Leech was to be killed, the "Chief" had ordered it—always they talked of the "Chief," never did they give him a name. I tried to pretend that there was hope even if it were my husband. I should have known better. I knew that Malone and his men were employed sometimes, that there was a policeman who gave information away; he had done so for several years. When it appeared that some policeman suspected it, it was decided to make out that you were the man. That satisfied superstition, as well. Malone introduced this policeman to Pickerell. I do not know who it is."

"Do you know where Pickerell is hiding?" Roger asked.

"No," said Mrs. Cartier.

"You're sure you've not heard the name of the policeman?"

"I have not," said Mrs. Cartier. She drew a deep breath. "Do you think he will come?"

"Yes."

The woman fell silent. Roger stepped to the window and looked out—and, after a few minutes, saw a taxi draw up. Close behind it there came a private car. He saw Sam and another of Morgan's men approaching, closing in as he had instructed. His jaw stiffened when he saw Abbott climb out of the second car with Tiny Martin. He could not see who was in the taxi, it drew up too close to the building. Abbott and Martin disappeared from his sight, another car, doubtless with Sloan inside, came down the street.

Morgan's men waited.

Roger turned and looked towards the door. The waiting seemed unending but at last there was a tap on the passage door; the maid opened it and a man stepped through.

"Is Mr. Cartier in?" he asked.

"No," said the maid, repeating a lesson, "but Madam is in."

"It doesn't matter," the man said and Roger's mouth dropped. He could not really believe the evidence of that voice. He knew it well, *but it was not Abbott's.* "As soon as your master returns, tell him to go north, as arranged. Do you understand? Tell him to go north. And tell him there is the possibility that someone will have to travel from Chelsea, also."

The maid said: "I will tell him."

"All right," said the man; his voice was unmistakable—it was *Cornish*!

Seeing him through a gap in the door Roger hardly recognized him, for Cornish had dyed his hair, was wearing a mackintosh with the collar turned up and looked disreputable. Only the voice condemned him. "Tell him to hurry," Cornish repeated.

There was a pause followed by a gasp.

"Look out, Martin!" Abbott called out.

Cornish pushed his way into this room, slammed the door, and demanded:

"Where's the back door?"

"It's no good, Cornish," said Roger.

The man swung round. His mouth gaped open, his hand seemed to sag in his pocket. There was a moment of utter silence before Cornish stiffened. Roger moved swiftly to one side, but he had never been more glad to see Tennant launch himself forward with his bewildering speed. Cornish fired once from his pocket, but the bullet hit the floor. Then he went down underneath Tennant, who kept his balance and stood over his victim. He put a heel on Cornish's wrist, forcing the gun away. Roger kicked it aside.

Mark opened the front door, to admit Abbott and Martin.

"Well?" Abbott said, flatly. He looked at Tennant's victim. "Is it Cornish?"

"Yes," Roger said gruffly.

"I was afraid so from the time Malone tried to escape. Only Cornish could have given him that key." It seemed an effort for Abbott to speak. "He went to Leech's public house but did not come out as himself. Martin and I thought he looked like Cornish. So we've reached the end of the hunt."

"Yes, it's over," said Roger heavily.

He realized that Cornish had been transferred comparatively recently from AZ Division. When on the Division itself, he had worked only in the East End, where he had ample opportunity to work with Malone. The failure to keep constant guard at Welbeck Street had been his responsibility. The time taken tracing Dixon was all explained. So was Malone's confidence.

Yet even the day when Cornish had been the first Yard man to offer him friendly help, Roger had not given him a thought.

It proved that Cornish had telephoned the Yard several times, and had eventually heard about Oliphant. He had acted quickly, not knowing that he himself was followed. No Yard men had been stationed at Bonnock House. Cornish had felt quite safe to come in person, when he discovered that Cartier's telephone was out of order.

Cornish tried to save himself by making a complete confession. That, the tapes and the other evidence made the case damning against all three men. Lois Randall had been a victim of circumstances, precipitated by her own lapse. Malone's part as the "strong man" of the organisation was fully disclosed; ordinary theft had gone on side by side with the distribution from the Society.

Pickerell had been the intermediary, approached by Cartier to handle the distribution. He had known Malone, and had linked the two organisations.

In Chatworth's office late that night, Roger told his part of the final story. Abbott was there, thin-voiced and aloof as ever.

"So we have it all," Chatworth said with deep satisfaction. "You didn't need to use Morgan's men very much, either. I must say you handled that part of it well; even without Abbott you would have got Cornish." He smoothed his hair, flattening it against the sides of his head. "What of Pickerell?"

"His body was found in Leech's public house," Abbott said.

"Do you know who killed him?"

"Malone did just before he left for Fulham. I think Pickerell was losing his nerve," said Abbott.

"I wouldn't be surprised," said Chatworth. "Well, West, you seem to have had the thick end of the stick most of the time. Not a nice story about Cartier. There's no case against his wife, though," Chatworth said. "Have you got the full story of the Cox murder?"

"Cornish says that Cox murdered his wife and that there was no motive apart from that we already knew," said Roger. "Oliphant defended Cox because he was afraid of what the man might say, but Cox only knew the Malone end of the organization. I once believed that Cox was drugged but I was wrong. He knew he would hang, anyhow, and saw no point in ratting on Malone. He believed that Malone was paying Oliphant, and so doing his best for him. Cox didn't know about Cornish. Only Malone, Pickerell and Cartier knew him."

"What about the Randall girl?"

"We know how she came to get mixed with them," said Roger. "I shouldn't think we could get a conviction even if we charged her."

"One of your troubles is that you're an incurable romantic," Chatworth growled. "Oh, you're right, West. One of these days you'll be right too often. It'll do you good to have a failure. Eh, Abbott?"

Abbott considered. "It might," he admitted, frostily.

Roger smiled. "Very good of you to say I've never had one, sir!"

"Eh?" barked Chatworth. He laughed. "All right, West, you'll do! I hear that you've got some tidying up on hand at your house. Oh, that reminds me—the taxi-driver, Dixon?"

Roger grimaced.

"He was used to try to make us concentrate on Mrs. Cartier and to head us off Cartier himself," he said. "I think it was that which first started me thinking of the man; Malone's effort to make Dixon implicate the woman was too clumsy. Malone was always too clever; I've never seen a man with such conceit."

"You won't see him much longer," Chatworth said. "All right, off with you!"

When Roger had gone, the AC looked thoughtfully at Abbott.

"What's your opinion of West?" he demanded.

"Much higher than it was a week ago, sir," said Abbott, with wry humour. "I always found it a trifle difficult to believe his guilt. I ought to say this, however. The money *was* left at his house. Morgan did take it away."

"Are you sure?"

"Yes," said Abbott. "The man who put it there has said so. Also, West asked a sergeant to trace two five-pound notes which proved to be two of two hundred sent by Leech on Malone's orders. Leech's prints were on some of the notes. The balance reached us by post this evening—the wrapping paper is bare of prints. I suspect that one of Morgan's men posted it, on West's instructions."

"Hum." Chatworth looked over his glasses. "Can we really prove it? And if we can, do we want to? Morgan has been very helpful."

Abbott smiled thinly. "I don't think we can and I don't think we should, sir."

"Then we agree," said the AC. "Well, you'll have to start clearing up, Abbott. Give West a couple of days to get over his home troubles, and then get him busy, too."

Roger meanwhile telephoned Wray and Tamperly, delighting the pressmen, and also made a comprehensive report. He was still in his office when Abbott telephoned to say that he need not come in for a day or two. Roger put on his hat and coat and left the Yard. He drove to Fulham, where he found Mark and Tennant sharing one spare room, the small room being occupied by Lois Randall who, said Janet, was asleep. Dixon had gone.

Janet was waiting in the dining-room. She looked a little tired and troubled. The wrecking had affected her far more than she had let Roger think, but she soon brightened up.

The *Echo* and the *Cry* and their associated evening papers gave the case enormous publicity. One of the Sunday newspapers tried to run a series of articles on Mrs. Cartier but failed because they could not get any information of great interest.

She gave her evidence, at the trial, against some of the men but not against her husband. She was in court when the jury returned the verdicts, the black cap was donned and the sentences were passed. Then she left. Outside, she saw Janet and Lois.

Janet smiled, uncertainly.

Mrs. Cartier approached, shook hands, and hurried off.

Soon afterwards Roger was able to tell her that the Society was working again, that Lois was reinstated as secretary but as Lois Tennant, no longer Lois Randall. Tennant was back in the north, finishing his Army service.

Mark said that nothing would ever satisfy the boisterous energy of that tough young man.

In midsummer a furniture van drew up outside the Bell Street house. Roger was at the Yard and Janet opened the door. She thought that there must be some mistake, until she read the note that the foreman remover had brought with him.

"Roger!" breathed Janet into the telephone, five minutes later. "Darling, it's incredible, but—Mrs. Cartier!"

"What about Mrs. Cartier?" asked Roger, startled.

"She's sent us *all* the furniture from the lounge at her Weybridge house. She is giving the place up. Darling, it's *twice* as good as anything we ever had! I know the sentimental value isn't the same but *do* you think you could get home early and help me put the room straight? And shall I ask Mark?"

"Yes, my sweet. And I'll be home by four sharp!" promised Roger.